Dr. Marcus Jones is world-famous for inventing a procedure to make cardiac surgery quicker and safer. He has achieved much in the ten years since he graduated from medical school, including accumulating more wealth than he had ever dreamed of growing up in the projects in Chicago. But he has not been as successful in his personal life. His lawyer wife is divorcing him — but then, he was never really in love with her. He has only felt that way about one woman — the one he dated back in college — the one who got away. When he finds her name on the internet, he contacts her, determined to see if he can rekindle what they once had together in college, back when he could only spare one night a week away from his studies and his world revolved around Tuesdays.

This book is a work of fiction. Names, characters, places, and incidents either are products of the author's imagination or are used fictitiously. Any resemblance to actual events or locales or persons, living or dead, is entirely coincidental.

Two for Tuesday
Copyright © 2021 Fiona McGier
ISBN: 978-1-4874-3195-2
Cover art by Martine Jardin

Published by eXtasy Books Inc or
Devine Destinies, an imprint of eXtasy Books Inc

Look for us online at:
www.eXtasybooks.com or www.devinedestinies.com

Two for Tuesday

By

Fiona McGier

DEDICATION

To Paul, who knows it's possible to tame a wild woman, because he did it.

CHAPTER ONE:-SHOULD HE, OR SHOULDN'T HE?

M arcus Jones didn't remember consciously planning to go to see her. He just realized all of a sudden, when the conference ended at noon, that it was a Friday afternoon and he had no appointments until Tuesday, and he was in the same state that she lived in. *Just how many hours would it take to get up there from Madison?* He had not yet checked out of his room, so he went back to it and turned on the laptop to get a map and directions. *Do they have directions to towns that small?*

He was surprised to find that it wasn't quite as tiny and inconsequential as he had imagined. In fact, compared to the other tiny dots along the highway, it was a fairly good-sized town. The directions seemed easy enough to follow, and the computer estimated time of arrival was three to four hours' drive time. Of course that was presuming one followed the speed limit. *Which I never do. Especially since my Jaguar does zero to eighty in a few seconds and purrs like a kitten while cruising at ninety. But will she agree to spend any time with me?*

He brooded. She'd said in her last e-mail that she didn't want to see him until his divorce was final. She was afraid of the repercussions of being an unmarried high school teacher seeing a married man, a big-city, world-famous cardiologist. She never mentioned his color. But then to her, that had never mattered. *Are there any Black people that far north in Wisconsin?*

Suddenly Marcus was blindsided with images of the light streaming in through the window next to her bed, illuminating her pale white skin next to his brown skin. Which led to remembering what they were doing at the time. He felt himself getting harder than he had in years. He smiled to himself, wondering if being with her again would allow him to perform as he used to do when they were together and both in their early twenties. He struggled against accepting it as inevitable that ten years would somewhat diminish his sexual cravings. But whenever he thought about her, they were as intense as they had ever been. *Still, is it worth it to drive all the way up there, when she might not even agree to spend any time with me? That is, presuming I can even find her.*

He remembered what it had been like for them back when they were at school together. He remembered when he met her — their first night together — all of the other times over their almost two years together. He remembered just how much pain he felt when she ended their relationship. Looking back, he understood why she had done it — but it still hurt. He had tried to forget about her. He dated other women — even convinced himself he was ready to marry someone else.

But from the minute he'd thought to check for her name on Facebook, he realized he'd been working up to this point. He found her and sent her a friend request. After an interminable wait, he had gotten an acceptance from her. Then he knew he would have to see her again, sometime. *Why not today?*

She told him not to come up until he was divorced. *Hey, it's in the works — only a matter of time. And when will I be only three to four hours away again, with no appointments or operations scheduled for three days?*

If I time it right, I'll get up there just as she's getting off of school for the weekend — a long, holiday weekend. I'll ask her out to dinner. Yes, just the thing. Dinner between two old friends from college — what could be more innocent?

He smiled at his own *very far from innocent* thoughts, and began to pack up the last of his things, including his notes and his laptop. He lugged it all down to his car before checking out of his room.

The clerk seemed surprised that he wasn't staying the weekend. Most of the doctors in for the convention were staying until at least Sunday.

She asked in an inviting tone, "Don't you want to stay around long enough to see the sights of downtown? I could show you around."

Amused that the young clerk might be trying to flirt with him, he politely turned down her offer and paid his bill, then left the building. *Honey, I'm old enough to be your daddy. Ew!*

The drive confirmed everything he had always thought about life away from the city. Lots of miles of nothing to look at. Nothing but corn fields, barns, and cows. *And what is that awful smell? Cow shit, or pig shit?* He always laughed at her, when she told him it was easy to tell the difference. She said that pig shit was unique—you knew that was what you were smelling when the aroma snuck right up into your nostrils and pulled the hairs out, making your eyes water. He just figured it all stank, so who cared what kind of animal made it? She told him that she was proud to be a farm girl, and he was just a big-city snob. They agreed to disagree, way back then.

Out here in the middle of the great big emptiness of Wisconsin farm fields, he remembered why he lived in the city of Chicago, with its hustle and bustle of life—human life, with human smells all around him. He turned up the CD even louder, as if hoping that the loud music of the city would somehow insulate him from the mile-after-mile of nothing that he was rapidly driving through. But each mile brought him closer to her, and that was the whole point of this. He speeded up, pushing closer to the limit of his car.

And since there was so little traffic on the road, compared to what he was used to on Lake Shore Drive, he allowed himself to reminisce about how he had met the only woman he had ever really loved.

Chapter Two:-Marcus Remembers
How it All Began

Marcus paid for his beer, cursing the fact that he never had enough left over to give the bartender a bigger tip. Beers were $1.75 on Tuesday nights, and he never could spare more than $2.00. One beer, once every two weeks, an hour or so to relax. Then he had to force himself back to his dorm room, like always, to slog back into his never-ending homework pile. He knew damn well that if he hadn't earned a full-ride scholarship, he would never have been able to even attend college. He was grateful. But he was also keenly aware that other students could piss around for a semester or two and still graduate—maybe a year or so late. He, on the other hand, had only one shot at getting his degree. And it depended on him continuing to get the highest possible grades he could—certainly nothing lower than a B.

He already had his BS in biology from this school. He was part-way into his medical graduate program, and the work level had become exponentially harder with each passing semester. He figured that an hour once every two weeks was about all he could give himself and still hope to keep up. He'd long ago accepted that his early schooling in the Chicago Public School system had not prepared him for the level of work expected here. Other students were not so surprised, or at least they had the cushion of knowing that they had help back home if they needed it. He had only his mother's prayers and the good wishes of some of the neighborhood folks, who hoped that his success would show the world that there were some smart people living in his part of the city.

Breathing a heavy sigh, he went back to his table to sit with the few guys he knew from his classes. Most of them spent a whole lot more time here, judging by the number of girls who frequently stopped by to chat. They looked curiously at the new guy, then walked on when he didn't have much to say to them.

What can I say? "Hi, I'm really lonely. I haven't been laid since – I don't even remember when. But all I can spare is an hour once every two weeks. So if you don't mind, let's go back to your place, screw, then I've got homework to get back to, okay?" Right! That's sure to turn off even the most curious of white girls who might have wanted to cross the color line for the first time. The black girls seem to know just how poor I am, so they aren't interested. So who does that leave? Wryly he looked at his right hand palm. *Nope, no hair yet, despite all I was taught in church.* He took another drink from his beer.

All of a sudden his reverie of self-pity was interrupted by some girls yelling.

"Is there a doctor in the house?"

"Does anyone know CPR? Or that other thingie?"

"She's choking, damn it! Doesn't anyone know what the hell to do?"

On auto-pilot, he jumped up and ran over to the table across the dance floor. Only a few people were dancing, since bands played there only on weekends. There a girl sprawled on the floor by a table, turning a bright shade of scarlet while she gasped, trying to get some air.

Just as he had been trained to do, he questioned her. "Are you choking?"

She nodded vigorously, while her girlfriends screamed helpful insults at him.

"Duh!"

"Are you blind or stupid?"

"Do something!"

He knelt behind her back, pushing her upright, and carefully placed his hands under her rib cage. He fisted them and pushed up. Once — twice — three times was the charm. A huge chunk of indistinguishable bar food flew across the floor. Immediately she was gasping in huge breaths of air, her color starting to change from the blue-ish color she had been turning back to scarlet, to red. Then she turned an embarrassed red shade, flushing on her white skin.

She turned to grab his arm to pull herself up to stand. Her voice was hoarse. "Thanks."

He smiled at her, handing her off to her friends. "You're welcome." He turned to go back to his table.

"Wait," she croaked. "What's your name? You saved my life!"

"Marcus. Marcus Jones. I'm studying to be a doctor, but you're the first person whose life I've saved. Thank *you*, for letting me know just how cool that feels!" Then he did walk away.

Her friends surrounded her, steadied her on her feet, and hustled her out of the door.

"Wow." The waitress appeared at his table, which still held his almost empty beer. She put another one in front of him.

"What's this? I didn't order another beer."

"No. But the bartender saw what you did. That's one of our regulars you just saved. If she stopped coming in, we'd probably go out of business!"

He stared at her.

She smiled at him. "No, really. This one's on the house."

Marcus smiled as he looked at his new beer. *This is the first time I've ever realized any profit from all of my hard work.* He gave himself permission to spend another hour in the bar, enjoying the fruits of his labors.

Two weeks later, Marcus walked into town again after dinner in the dorm and used what little profit he had left-over from his twice-monthly government-issued living expenses check to buy himself a beer. He looked around for familiar faces to sit with. When he didn't see any, he sought out an open chair and sat down at a table by himself. He was just starting his regular habit of brooding over his lot in life when one of the most beautiful women he had ever seen crossed the dance floor, staring directly at him.

How can she manage to walk and move her hips like that without spilling any of her beer? Her smile says she knows she looks like a wet-dream walking. What the hell does she want from me? His long-ignored desires flared to life. He was incapable of coherent thought while the blood rapidly abandoned his brain.

"Hi. You're Dr. Marcus, aren't you?" She smiled at him as if she already knew the answer.

"Uh, yeah. I'm Marcus. But I'm not a doctor yet." He was grateful that his dark skin would hide the blush he could feel creeping up his body as he responded to her overwhelming sexuality.

"Well, I'm Melanie. You saved my life a couple of weeks ago, remember?" She pantomimed choking, while grasping her throat with both hands.

"I remember."

"Can I sit down? Thanks." She oozed into the chair next to Marcus and scooted it closer to him.

"You know," she leaned forward conspiratorially. "You're really hard to find. No one knows much about you. You don't come in very often, and I barely remember the name you said, since I was kind of—you know—out of it? My friends were too busy dragging me home to party, to help me forget my near-brush with death. I've been asking everyone who might know you just who you are, and how I could get in touch with you. Mike—you know, the bartender there? He said he gave you a beer *on the house* for saving one of his best customers, so they didn't have to close the joint. Ha ha. Big comedian, that guy. He said you only come in every couple of weeks. He thought it was always on a Tuesday. Well, since I only live a couple of blocks away, I'm in here almost every night. If I have a theme paper due the next day, then I'm up all night researching and writing. I'm an English major. Did I mention that? Anyway, I knew I'd see you in here again sooner or later. So I've been watching for you every night, and now here you are!" She smiled triumphantly at him.

Stunned, Marcus just stared, not sure if a response was called for.

"So," she continued. "You know, I *do* breathe every now and then, and that's your cue to talk if you want to. But if you don't, that's okay too. I'll just keep on talking. Anyway, I wanted to think of something I could do to really thank you for saving my life and all. If I could cook, I'd make you dinner. But I'm not really very good in the kitchen. If I could bake, I'd make you cookies—but ditto there. I don't know you well enough to write you a poem. Besides, that's really cheesy, considering you saved my life and all. But there *is* something I'm really good at." She paused, really looking at him, studying him, as if he were a bug under a microscope.

He shifted around in his seat, trying to unobtrusively adjust himself without using his hands,

"You're kind of a quiet guy, aren't you?"

He nodded, still unable to make words come out. His cock throbbed angrily against the zipper of his jeans, accusing him of neglect. The smell of her perfume and her skin was intoxicating him, and he was afraid that if she leaned any closer, he wouldn't be able to stop himself from throwing her across the table and tearing her clothes off. He tried not to stare at her erect nipples that were threatening to tear holes in her tee shirt. But he was still blushing from what he was imagining, so it was difficult to look her in the eye.

"But you *are* kind of cute, in an under-fed, nerdy kind of way. Tell you what, dude. What I'm *really* good at is screwing. In fact I'm trying to get the college to let me minor in it." She gave him a mischievous grin.

His jaw dropped open.

"So, if you're up for it, let's finish our beers. Then we can stroll back to my place, where I conveniently have more beer in the fridge. Then I can *really* thank you for saving my life. How's that?"

Marcus would not have thought it possible for his cock to get even harder than it already was. But it twitched and throbbed as he imagined burying himself between her thighs. *Have I died and gone to Heaven? I don't remember an accident — but this can't be real! Here is one of the best-looking women I've ever seen up close, with long, wavy brown hair with red streaks, and pale skin with freckles on her face. I wonder just how much of her body is covered with freckles?*

She was thin, but not too thin to have nice tits, nice hips — and the heat radiating off of her was burning him even though they were barely touching. She wasn't expecting him to buy her dinner, or even to buy her a drink. She was offering to have sex with him, with no strings attached. In fact her hazel eyes were sparkling across the table at him, daring him to refuse her.

"So, what do you say, Marcus? We on, or not? Or do you need more time to think about it?"

"Uh — um. Can I finish my beer first?"

"Sure." She grinned. "I don't like to waste it either."

"Um. So you're an English major, huh?" He figured if he got her talking again, he would have time to analyze the situation. Or at least to wrestle some blood back from his cock for his brain to process what she was offering.

"Yea, I talk a lot, in case you hadn't noticed. And I love to read and then write about what I think about what I read. In fact, I write all the time — stories, poetry, song lyrics, etc.

About the only homework I really like to do is my English homework, so that's what I'm majoring in. My parents are really pissed at me, telling me that I'll starve to death with an English degree. They want me to pick something that I can make a lot of money with, to pay them back for their help with my tuition and stuff. I have a part-time job, but I spend a lot of *that* money in here. Actually, that's my diet plan in a nutshell. I eat when I go home to see the folks. Otherwise I eat when I can spare some beer money." She paused to take a breath, looked at him expectantly.

He gulped his beer.

"So, you're a med student? That's how you knew what to do to save my ass?"

"Yea. Yours is the first life I've ever saved. You know, the work is so hard and there's so much of it that I sometimes wonder if it's worth it. But I've felt so good ever since I did the Heimlich for you that I guess if I can feel that good for a living, saving people and all, then it will be worth it, right?" *Is that her hand on my knee? Now it's moving up to my thigh? Oh Lord have mercy. Honey, stop or I'll blow here and now!*

"Uh — yeah. Marcus, you about done with that beer?"

He chugged the last quarter of it in one swallow.

"Let's hit the road and get to my place. The beer's cold, the woman is hot, and my roommate is at her boyfriend's place for the night. Let's go party!"

Pulling him up by the hand, she led him out the door, into the cool night air.

They walked along in silence for the two blocks to her street. They had to stop to wait for the light to change. Melanie took that moment to press herself against him, grabbing his neck and pulling his face down to kiss her.

Not sure how to react, Marcus tried to remain cool. But she was insistent, pushing her tongue into his mouth, moaning when he responded, wiggling to fit herself against him more fully, rubbing herself against his increasingly painful erection.

When the light changed, she pulled away. Her voice was husky in its urgency. "Let's get to my place now!"

I'll follow you anywhere, honey. Just so you touch me again.

Climbing the stairs to her apartment seemed to take forever. There were three apartments at the top of the stairs. She went to the door on the left and unlocked the door. He followed her into the tiny apartment and looked around. Feeling even more awkward now that they were alone together, Marcus waited for a cue from her as to what she expected.

"Go on and sit on that couch over there, Marcus. I'll grab us a couple of beers and be there in a sec."

He stood rooted to the spot, unable to move.

She grabbed a bag of taco chips along with a jar of salsa and moved over to the couch, patting the cushion next to her as an invitation. "Come on and sit over here by me, Marcus. I promise not to bite—that is, unless you ask me really nicely, and promise to bite me back!" She giggled.

This must be a dream. I hope I don't wake up. He forced his legs to move him over to the couch and sat down.

She tossed her hair back, as she grabbed the remote to turn on the stereo. "What's your pleasure, big guy?"

He gulped.

"Music, I mean."

"Oh." He perched uneasily on the opposite end of the couch. "Anything you like is okay with me."

"Blues it is, then." The sounds of Buddy Guy's guitar filled the room.

"What, because I'm Black, you think I like the blues?" He tried not to sound like he had the chip on his shoulder that he rarely acknowledged.

"No, silly. Black folks don't like the blues anymore. I guess they figure they live them, so no need to listen to them. Or maybe they don't like them anymore because white people do. I like them, and you told me to put on what I want. So there."

She moved closer to Marcus. "Are you afraid of me? Or just nervous? Do you want to get high first? Or are you too *doctor-y* to smoke anything?"

Marcus closed his eyes to take a deep breath. He turned to face her, trying to keep the neediness out of his voice. "I don't really know why I'm here. You don't know anything about me, yet you asked me up here. What's the deal? You wanting to cross the color line and I looked like a good candidate? Cause that's okay, if that's all it is. But I just need to know." *God, I sound like an idiot!* He was shaking with nerves and sexual need, and in imminent danger of losing what little control he was fighting to exert over himself.

She peered at him closely before sighing heavily. "Men! You all say you want sex with no commitments, but when it gets offered freely, you're all questioning and wondering what the hell is going on. It's like you want it, but when you don't have to work for it, you don't. You guys need to make up your minds. It's confusing for a girl. Especially one who likes sex as much as I do. And as for the color-line? Dude, I've been across and back a few times already. It's not true what they say—some of us go back and forth. But I don't screw guys for their color. I pick guys I like—guys I want to have sex with—then I invite them up here. You have even more of a right to be here than anyone else I've ever invited up, since if you hadn't saved my ass, I wouldn't be able to screw anyone anymore!" She moved closer to him on the couch.

"I'd probably have tried to seduce you sooner or later anyway. I just never noticed you in the bar before. To tell you the truth, I don't usually go there on Tuesdays. My only late class is six to eight on Tuesday, so unless I want to eat during *the old folks hour*, before my class, I don't have time for dinner. That's why I was snarfing so heavily when I choked on that gross bar food. You saved my life, then didn't even wait around for me to thank you properly. By the time I had my breath back, I was here and there was a hellacious party going on. And none of those bitches thought to invite you. I mean really, you shoulda been the guest of honor! Boy was I pissed! Then I had a hell of a time finding someone who knew who you were. And then I had to go every night at about the same time to see when you would show up. I felt like a goddamned stalker!" She glared at him, as if to blame him for not being easier to find.

"I felt kinda weird about my offer, because it seemed to weird you out. But not so much that you didn't leave the bar with me. That means either of two things. Either you never get any, in which case, I'm going to blow your socks off. Or you really think I'm hot, but you don't know if you should trust me by being here. News flash — you can trust me. You're safe up here. And either way, I'm going to blow your socks off!"

She took another drink from her beer before setting the bottle down and turning to him. She reached out to take one of his tightly clenched hands into hers.

"Trust me, this isn't any kind of set-up, and I have no hidden agenda. There's no strings attached — honest. I just like to fuck. I've got condoms, beer and snacks to last all night, and no one's going to bother us. So why don't we get to work making some dreams come true?" She leaned over and pressed herself against the front of him and kissed him again, tongue exploring his mouth, sucking on his tongue when he slid it into her mouth. She slid her hands under his tee shirt and moaned before leaning back and pulling it off. She kissed his neck, then trailed her tongue down his chest, inhaling the scent of his skin, rubbing her face on him, sucking gently on one nipple, then the other. Her hands were busy too, rubbing him through his pants.

Marcus lost his battle with his cock. *I'm going to take her up on her offer. As if there was ever any doubt!* He slid his hands up under her shirt to tease her pebbled nipples.

She moaned again, before helping him to pull her shirt off. *No bra! Which one do I suck on first?*

She leaned against him, rubbing her nipples against his chest, letting him feel how hard they were.

I'm not really here. But damn, what a dream! He'd been with women before, even a couple of white ones. But none as willing as this one, and none so sensual. He had always enjoyed them—their scent, their soft flesh, their heat. But he had never been made to feel like *he* was a sex object. This woman was devouring him, tasting him all over, smelling him, dragging her tongue all over him, like she was a cat who wanted to scent-mark him. And she was just as anxious to get him naked as he was to strip her. She was encouraging him to explore her as well, and he realized that anything he wanted to do with her would be okay.

He reached deeply into himself, for his big-dick mojo. *Okay, honey. It's show-time. Time to be the best lay you've ever had!*

She worked her way down his body, licking and biting him, tiny love nibbles that would probably leave marks on the more sensitive places that made him jump when she bit down. He lifted his butt up to help her pull his pants off. He helped her by kicking off his shoes. After tossing his pants aside, she tore his socks off. When she moved her mouth up to his rock-hard cock, he almost laughed, remembering her promise to *blow his socks off.* But laughter was the last thing he was capable of once her mouth closed around him.

She explored him slowly, licking up and down the length of him. She buried her face in the hair around his balls, fondling them gently, using her hands to caress them, while her tongue drove him mad, making him slick with her saliva. When she looked up at him, she smiled at the dreamy look on his face.

He knew his eyes were unfocused, his hands clutching at

the pillows around him.

She sucked the head into her mouth, clamping her lips down on him. Her tongue swirled around, its tip poked into the slit that was weeping tears of joy for her. She used the flat top of her tongue to stimulate the crease along the outside of his cock, before suddenly swallowing him whole.

He stopped breathing. *Is that the back of her throat?*

She stopped for just a quick second, regaining control over her gag reflex. Then she resumed licking and sucking him as if his engorged cock was an all-day sucker that she wanted to finish in an hour.

Marcus gasped as she took him farther and farther down her throat each time, showing off for him how good she was at giving head. When his cock wasn't buried to the hilt in her throat, she moaned, wriggling her ass as if the act of cock-sucking aroused her. He tried to hold himself back, but the insistent sucking, the wet tongue swirling around on him, and the sounds she was making, along with the sight of her beautiful tits as they bounced around with her movements, rubbing on his thighs, made him unable to hold back the orgasm that had already been long over-due before they even started. He tried to warn her that his explosion was imminent but couldn't force any words out of his throat before the spasms began. He felt his balls squeeze up to his body, the force shooting up with such intensity he was afraid he would choke her.

Melanie clearly anticipated what was happening. At the first twitch of his orgasm, she backed off so as not to be hit in the back of her throat. The hot load shot into her mouth and she smiled as she used her hands, one still fondling his balls, the other milking him with sure strokes. What didn't get swallowed by her was shot onto her face and her hand. Marcus groaned, lifting himself up off the couch cushion as he came. He collapsed back down into a boneless satisfied heap, his breathing ragged as he tried to take in enough oxygen to slow his heartbeat.

She reached under the couch and pulled out a box of tissues, which she used to mop them both off. She moved up onto the couch next to Marcus, who was still panting. She grabbed her own beer and took a few swallows before leaning over to kiss him, her tongue making lazy circles on his lips. "You ready for your beer yet? Or are you still trying to catch your breath?"

Marcus smiled at her weakly, lifting a shaking arm to grasp the beer she handed to him. He took a long drink, then pushed himself up straighter. She leaned back on the couch and put her feet up on the table in front of them. They spent a few moments sipping beer before Marcus felt able to speak. "My turn?"

She nodded at him. He leaned over and kissed her lips, forcing his tongue into her mouth, tasting himself along with the beer. Their tongues dueled as he explored her body with his hands. He gently tugged and pulled on first one nipple then the other, while his other hand moved into her hair to grasp it firmly on the back of her head. She began to moan softly, moving her hips in reaction to his touches. He traced a path down her stomach and stopped kissing her long enough to look down at the tiny tattoo of a smiling cat's face under her belly button. He looked back at her and was aroused by the expression of lust on her face. He pressed his lips to hers again as they took turns sucking on each other's tongues.

His hand continued its exploration as he slid it down into the front of her pants. She moaned when his finger pushed down into her curls and found the hood over her clit. He pressed gently on it, then pulled his hand out to use both hands to undo the front of her jeans. She had obviously kicked off her sandals at some point, but he had no idea when. He got onto his knees on the floor in front of her and pulled off her pants, then gently massaged her feet, up her legs to her thighs, then to her messy curls. He traced along her thighs from her knees with his tongue, leaning forward to inhale deeply before beginning at the other knee and licking up that thigh also. She was shifting around on the couch, thrusting her hips forward, while he took his time in tasting all around his ultimate goal.

She moaned again. "Marcus, please—"

He used his thumbs to spread her apart and he attacked her clit, the center of her pleasure. He licked and sucked from her clit to her hole, then back again. She began to keen, a wailing sound, bucking beneath him, helpless in her pleasure, her voice rising and falling with the strength of successive orgasms.

She came already? And again? Wonder how long I can keep her screaming? He learned what pleased her by how hard she bucked against him and how much noise she made. He enjoyed making her come and watching her face. He noticed a red flush creeping all over her body.

When she appeared to lose the ability to scream and just began to pant and moan, he moved up to sit next to her, to drink some of his beer and eat some chips. He really was hungry. All appetites were aroused by this woman, so he chomped quickly to revive his energy while she recovered from his attention. She sucked down her beer, then thoughtfully chewed a couple of chips. She recovered quickly.

Soon she was rubbing his increasingly hard erection with a steady, experienced hand. She paid attention to what made him merely squirm and what made him moan. She moved onto his lap, straddling his thighs, and pulled a condom out from the cushions. She rolled it onto him, then rubbed the head of his shaft against herself, as if trying to decide if the time was right yet. Just when he thought she was making him so crazed that he would have to ram himself into her whether she was ready or not, she dropped herself onto him, taking his length into herself with one movement, and with a shriek, she came.

Like a wild man he bucked, thrusting himself into her as if he couldn't get deep enough. Despite what she'd said about frequent sex, her passage was tighter and wetter than anything he had ever encountered. She felt like moist silk as she gripped him with muscles that squeezed the whole length of him. He dug his fingers into her hips, helping her to move in ways that gave them both optimal pleasures.

Long before he wanted to, he felt the pressure building at the base of his spine. His balls drew up tight to his body, then he exploded into her. He howled like a wild man as he came with an intensity he had never felt before.

Her muscles gripped him, their spasms making her come repeatedly. Each squeeze milked more out of him—each spurt made her come again.

This must be what a multiple orgasm feels like! Marcus felt a smile play on his lips as he wrapped his arms around her panting body while she lay on him, her head on his shoulder, her ragged breaths tickling the skin of his neck. He gave a long sigh—a sound of supremely satisfied male contentment.

Sometime between the couch and the bathtub, they used up another condom before retiring to soak their tired muscles in the steamy hot water while they talked, getting to know each other. Afterward they crawled into bed to cuddle and then reached for more condoms. Talking, laughing and sharing themselves with each other, they didn't fall asleep until the morning light was already streaming into the apartment.

When her alarm went off at eight am, Melanie hit it off immediately.

Marcus jumped up, apologizing for needing to hurry off to catch the bus back to the dorms so he could get to his nine am class.

Groggily she watched him dress. When he was ready to

leave, she got up to walk, naked and unselfconscious, across the room to kiss him goodbye.

She's a goddess! The light streaming in the window made her skin appear translucent, like she was glowing. The red in her hair, the green and yellow of her eyes, the freckles that he now knew were all over her body — all seemed to burn themselves into his consciousness. He felt like the luckiest man in the world. And yet he was also the most bereft, as he forced himself to walk out of her door. *I may never see you again, honey, but I'll never forget you!*

Marcus was deep into his homework a week later. His roommate was already asleep, having pulled two successive all-nighters in order to pass his most recent tests. Marcus was studying with the light shaded, trying to see, but really having to force himself to concentrate. He knew it was Tuesday night, and he also knew that he had no money this week. *She probably wouldn't care. She'd either buy me a beer or offer me one back at her place. But I can't go into the bar with no money. And what if I show up at her place and she has a man up there already?*

He sighed, trying to concentrate on mitochondrial DNA and the role it played in proving evolutionary theories. *Don't think about her breasts with those hard nipples. Don't think about how she smells — how she tastes — or how she looks when she arches her back from an orgasm that I gave her.*

He realized that he was hard again, that he was sweating profusely, and that there was someone knocking on his door. Swearing under his breath at his situation, he stalked over to the door and swung it open, expecting to see someone wanting to borrow his calculator. In his current mood, he was ready to be belligerent with the intruder.

"Hi-ya Marcus! I know it's Tuesday night, but not the right one for you, right? Well, I just got a check in the mail from my folks because I told them I needed a couple more books. I downloaded one of them as an e-book and borrowed the other one from a friend. Thus I find myself with a little bit of extra cash. *What can I do with this extra money?* I asked myself. Then, thinking altruistically of course, I remembered that you're so skinny because the food in the dorms sucks so bad. Yeah, I remember. My acne acts up just thinking about eating here. Yuck! No one wants to live here past freshman year. The fact that you *have* to just bites the big one. So anyway, I thought of you and your big — you know — appetite!"

She smiled at him in a wicked way, licking her lips, letting him know just what she had been thinking about. "So how about you and I take a stroll down to the Pizza Pit and split a pitcher of beer and a pizza? The surest way to know if you're compatible with someone is what kind of shit you like on your pizza, right? I mean, like if you wanted dead fish or anything gross like that, I'd either have to dump your ass immediately, or at least make you bring a toothbrush along, so you could brush before I kiss you again. Which reminds me —" She pasted herself to the front of him, twining one of her legs up and around behind his ass, wrapping her arms around him, and pulled him down for a very long, arousing kiss.

After a few sweaty moments, during which he wondered if his sleeping roommate would notice if he dragged her into his room and nailed her against the wall just to *take the edge off*, she pushed him back.

"Phew! Even better than I remembered. Marcus, you da man. I knew you were good enough to drag back to my bed for another round. Let's go eat. Food first — then each other for the rest of the night. Okay?" She smiled as she licked up his neck, rubbing herself against him. "You coming?"

"Honey, you keep kissing me like that, and I *will* be before we even get out of my doorway!" His hands lingered over her curves, tracing them like a blind man reading Braille — remembering, stroking, kneading, and needing.

"Hey, don't call me *honey*, okay? I knew this guy in high

school, a real alpha-asshole, and that's what he used to call me all the time. Like I was some damn bee-vomit. That's what honey is, you know. Ew! Gross! Grab your jacket, your wallet, whatever, and let's go!"

Grinning, feeling like the world was not such a cold place after all, he grabbed his jacket, his IDs, and his keys before following her out the door and into the night.

They had pizza with toppings they could both live with. *Thank God, since I forgot to bring a toothbrush.*

They finished their pitcher of beer and headed out the door, walking towards the bus stop. Marcus stopped suddenly and grabbed Melanie close for a lingering kiss, promising passion, suddenly desperate to taste her again.

"Hey, what's up? I thought we were in a hurry to get back to my place. Hence, the bus stop is next. But you want to make out here? Okay."

"It's just that I'm not sure I can walk that far with a hard-on this big." He moaned, placing her hand over it, feeling frenzied when she rubbed it up and down.

"Oooh, yeah, I can tell. Well, Marcus, we have two choices—no, three, really. We can try to get you to walk that far, but that's not really a good option now, is it? Or I can pull you over into the shadows of the bleachers over there and give you the best blow job you ever had."

He sucked in his breath before letting out a pained moan.

"Or three—we can head into the shadows for some hot, wild-monkey sex, and hope that we don't get caught. What do you think? Or is there too little blood in your brain for that pesky thinking-thing?"

He let her lead him into the shadows of the bleachers. He opened his jeans and slid them down.

Melanie pulled hers completely off of one leg, then smiled at him with a challenge in her eyes.

He slid a finger into her and found that the excitement of the moment had already gotten her wet enough. He quickly tore the top off the condom package she handed him and slid it on, then leaned into her and slid himself into her slick tightness, making them both moan with pleasure. They found a rhythm that allowed them to remain standing up, yet kept him sliding in and out, bringing her to a quick orgasm that almost made her scream. Apparently not wanting to make that much noise and risk being caught, she bit his shoulder, gnawing at him while he thrust into her again and again. He picked her up, holding her ass in his hands, and drove himself in until he groaned his release and his legs almost collapsed.

She slid down to the ground to stand in front of him, hugging him, partially holding him up. She smiled up at him and caressed his face with her hand while pulling off the condom with her other hand. She knotted it and put it into her pocket to dispose of later.

"Now can we go back to my place, you big stud?"

Unable to talk yet, he nodded weakly.

"I've missed you. I've missed your cock. So I'm not taking *No* for an answer. Let's go."

Many hours later, once again in the tub, Marcus sighed with pleasure while he rubbed her shoulders. Her ass was snug in between his thighs, and he could feel himself hardening as he pressed into her backside.

"You know Marcus, I've been thinking." She sounded hesitant.

What on earth can be causing her to sound so unsure of herself? She's the most supremely confident woman I've ever met — and with good reason. She's the best at anything she puts her mind to. I'm just grateful that she has her mind on me.

"I'm usually a one-time gal. I have that kind of reputation, which I nurture most carefully, so guys won't feel dissed when I won't let them in here again. Most guys are pretty disappointing between the sheets, but it can be problematic to tell them that—you never know how they'll react. Just like you never know how they're gonna be in the sack until you get them there. Good looks, great promise — then you get them naked and either they're convinced that their dick is so huge that you should fall on the floor in paroxysms of orgasm just looking at the size of it, or they are smaller and they work harder to please. But most men don't really want to listen to what I *want*. They just want to do some kind of generic *woman-pleasing thing*. You can almost see them remembering page-by-page, where to grab, and for how long. They get so disgruntled when I'm not screaming out the big O instantly. Sheesh! What a drag!"

"Then why keep on screwing us when you're usually so disappointed?" He was genuinely curious.

"Because I can, that's why!" She chuckled back at him. "Men have to work hard to get laid, as you well know. But all I have to do is let some guy know I'm interested, and I'm guaranteed to get him into my bed. Or his bed. Or his car — or wherever. It's like shooting fish in a barrel — it's almost too easy. But I really like orgasms. I'm totally hetero, so I love everything physically about men. Combine those two loves of mine, and I'm lucky I get any homework done at all."

"All this talking about getting laid is getting me hard again." He felt the need to point that out to her, just in case she might have missed the cannon attempting to poke its way into her backside.

"I did kind of notice that. But what I was getting around to is I really like having *you* in my bed. How's about we make it an *every Tuesday night* thing? You come on out to the bar, and I'll meet you there after my class. If it's an *I've got money today* day for you, fine. Buy a beer before I get there. If it's not, wait for me and I'll buy. We can eat something, sooner or later, or maybe we'll just drink. But that way, I'll know that at least one day of the week I'm going to be pleasured most excellently by a master. What do you think of my idea?" She turned in the water, sat on her heels, and looked into his face for a response.

He knew his face reflected shock, awe, and disbelief.

"Well?" She stroked his chest, his thighs, his shoulders.

"I'm speechless. Right now my dick is so hard I can hardly think, because what you're offering me is a wet dream come true. I don't have any money or time to woo any women, so I haven't been getting any for a long time. I figured that was going to be my life until I get out of medical school. Maybe even all the way until I get done with my residency. In fact, I've pretty much resigned myself to the fact that I'll be too fucking busy and tired to worry about *getting any* regularly, until I'm a rich and famous cardiologist. And probably by then I'll be too damn old to even get it up."

She looked into his eyes, teasing him. "You haven't been getting any practice? This is all just natural talent? Wow."

He sighed. "But then you come into my life, drag me into your bed, and make me experience pleasure way better than anything I ever imagined. And now instead of tossing me aside, as your *carefully-nurtured reputation* says you will, you're offering me a place in your bed weekly. A dependable night when I can relieve my tension, talk to someone who's funny and thoughtful, who listens when I talk, and at least seems to be interested. And I don't have to do anything but make love to you, which is the best thing that's ever happened to me! You even fed me tonight. Good God, girl, is there nothing I can do to thank you? Buy my own condoms? Learn the entire Kama Sutra, and practice it all with you? I'm yours for any time you'll give me. You can do anything you want with me. The rest of the week, I'll just exist, studying my ass off, working twice as hard as usual. But I'll know that Tuesday is coming soon, and then I will be, too."

He cupped both of her breasts in his hands. "In fact, if we keep on like this, you just might single-handedly be the most important part of my *support system* in getting me through medical school." He smiled at the thought. "Though I have no idea how I'll manage to thank you from the stage when I graduate, without shocking the hell out of the crowd."

She gave him a wicked smile. "Stress-relief? Relaxation-expert? Best lay ever?" With a naughty smile, holding his engorged organ with both hands, she lowered her head to lick off the drops leaking out of him, as he anticipated pleasures yet to be. "So, do you agree to my proposal?"

He groaned. "Yes!" He wrapped his hands in her hair as she took him in her mouth. They splashed what was left of the cooling water all over the floor, before heading back into the bedroom for the rest of that Tuesday night.

For the rest of that semester, they both came to depend on Tuesday nights. No matter how rotten the rest of the week was going, they knew they would see each other then, so it was possible to bear anything.

Melanie's roommate decided that Tuesday nights weren't any fun in their apartment, since she had to listen to their moaning and screaming all night. They also used up all of the hot water on baths. Plus she had to wait until they were done in the tub to pee. She moved a toothbrush into her boyfriend's apartment and took to staying there on Tuesdays. Life took on a semblance of routine, but all too soon the semester ended.

Marcus had gone home all of the previous summers, since his scholarship allowed for him to have gaps in his classes. But this time, after learning that Melanie had a job lined up for the summer and was staying in DeKalb, he applied for the summer Observation Seminar, which would have him shadow various doctors around, watching how they interacted with their patients, learning just what the life of a doctor entailed. Of course he was also expected to take additional classes. But this would earn him some extra credits and shave part of a semester off of his requirements. This meant he would be able to graduate in the spring, instead of having to take the additional time originally necessary, since he had been so far behind in his reading and writing skills. He convinced his counselor to approve his summer proposal.

Since the dorms were mostly unoccupied for the summer, he had to move into the sole wing still open. There would be no food served, he was told, but he would be given a small weekly allowance to enable him to eat enough to survive. *No problem. I'll add it to what Melanie earns, and that way I can contribute to the food bill.*

Melanie was thrilled to learn that Marcus was staying around for the summer. "There's mighty slim pickins around here for the summer. Last summer I was here and only managed to get laid a few times all summer. Very few men stayed around for the break, and the ones who were here were mostly attached to some woman who kept them on a tight leash. Now all we have to do is convince my roommate that she needs to spend more time with her boyfriend, and we can commence with the unadulterated fucking."

Marcus laughed, then indulged himself by screwing her hard and fast.

Her screaming made the neighbors pound on the wall and yell at them. "Shut the hell up in there unless you're being killed! If you *are* being killed, thank God! It'll finally be quiet around here!"

Marcus was a little worried about that. "What if they call the cops?"

Melanie smirked. "When all of your neighbors lived on the same dorm floor with you, you don't have to take anything they say seriously."

The summer passed quickly, since being with Melanie took up all of his down time. Marcus barely managed to pass his classes with high-enough grades. Fortunately his professors took pity on him, knowing him from previous classes. They cut him the slack he needed, letting him do extra credit toward the end of the summer. With their help, he got the grades he needed to keep his scholarship.

Melanie informed him that since this was her senior year, she would have to work harder than she had before. Not that this would cut into Tuesday nights. But for the spring semester, she would be student-teaching. That would have to take precedence over anything else, or she wouldn't graduate on time.

Grateful that she would be in the same situation that he was, Marcus told her that they would find a way to make things work. *We have to. I don't even want to think about what will happen when we leave DeKalb. I'm afraid that I'll wake up to find that you're just a wonderful dream.*

With the start of a new school year, there was a new crop of students, and hence a new crowd to hang out in all of the bars. Marcus found himself feeling more and more jealous of the various men that Melanie would entertain on the nights he was doing homework. On the second Tuesday night of the school year he told her as much, while they were still in the bar, having their one beer.

"So, what are you trying to do? Cramp my style? Clip my wings? Get me to commit to monogamy, which I don't even believe in, when I can only see you once a week? What the hell am I supposed to do the other nights of the week? Play with a vibrator?" She was getting more heated as she ranted. The flush that always crept up into her face when she was excited turned him on so much that Marcus almost forgot what they were talking about.

"Um — no." He leaned toward her. "What I'm proposing is that we add a weekend night to our schedule — maybe Friday or Saturday night. I really want a night with a day off of school after it, so I can stay in bed late into the morning with you. Like we did sometimes in the summer, remember? So I can wake up next to you and make love to you with the morning sun in your eyes. So I can pretend that you're *my girl*. Is that really too much to ask?"

Melanie shook her head. "You don't have to pretend Marcus. You know when you're here, I'm your girl. What you're really asking me to do is give up other men, right?"

Marcus cupped her face in his hand and leaned over to kiss her, sliding his tongue into her mouth, hungrily exploring while he considered what to say next. "Maybe not all of them, honey." He smiled when she flinched. "Maybe I'd just like more than one night a week with you, since you are so important to my peace of mind. Maybe I just want to feel that you belong to me, just a little bit. Maybe I'm falling so much in love with you that the thought of sharing you with other men is starting to really bother me. I don't know."

She sighed heavily. "Marcus—Marcus. Don't you know how much I care about you? I've *never* committed to a steady night with anyone before. I just spent the whole summer with *just you*. Admittedly, some of the very best sex I've ever had! Especially noteworthy because I didn't even have time to miss you in-between. And still I found myself lusting after you all day, until my minimum-wage crap-job was over, and I could find you and screw your brains out. But I'm not ready to be a monogamous-kind of gal yet. Next thing I know you'll be wanting to get married, or some such bullshit. I'm not in college to earn a *Mrs.*, you know. I want to work in my field, to teach. That's why I'm here. If I never get a chance to do that, then I'll have just been beating off all of this time, wasting all of my parents' and my own money."

He sat back, dejected

She leaned forward and took his face into her hands to look him in the eyes. "Would it make that look of pain go away if I agree to a weekend night also? Better yet, how about if we agree that as long as you call me and let me know when you're going to come over, that I'll be at your beck and call? I'd really rather fuck you than most of the men in the bars anyway. You satisfy me like no one else can. Will that make you happy?"

Marcus wasn't sure how to respond. He was almost unable to talk, since her hand was on his erection, holding him, stroking him, trying to convince him that since she was his *now*, that everything was all right with the world. "What if I can't get you on the phone, and I come into the bar and you're with someone else?"

"Then I'll ditch him and drag you home with me."

"Promise?" He was aware of how needy he sounded, but he didn't care.

"Of course." She wriggled her eyebrows up and down at him in a leer. "Now can we go to my place and — uh — shake on this, like honorable folks?"

Unable to resist her any longer, and able to convince himself that he'd scored a success, he agreed. As always, he knew he would follow her anywhere.

Shaking his head as his thoughts returned to the present, Marcus was pleasantly surprised to check his mileage and see that he was almost to his destination, much quicker than he had thought he would be. His memories had distracted him from most of the boring scenery. And knowing that he would see her again soon made him press his foot on the gas pedal just a little bit harder. The rolling green hills of central Wisconsin were passing by almost in a blur, while he smiled with anticipation.

CHAPTER THREE: UNEXPECTED VISITOR FOR MELANIE

M elanie McKee wearily carried the last box of files out to the faculty parking *Why the hell are the closest spots to my classroom reserved for students only? I've got to trek clear over to the other end of campus to get to my truck. I'm the employee here. Don't I count?*

She stopped twice to readjust her load. The box loaded with papers to grade wasn't so much heavy as bulky. Her shoulder bag held her lunch bag, her cell phone, her laptop, and the two books she had promised herself to read over the long weekend in order to be able to grade some of the reports she had in the box of files she carried.

Whenever she assigned book reports, she tried to stick to only books she had read, even if she hadn't read them since high school or college, so at least she could tell if they had read the whole book or not. But inevitably there were always one or two students determined to do their *favorite book in the whole world, Ms. McKee.* Sucker that she was, she always agreed to let them indulge themselves, even if it meant that she had to skim the damn things before she could grade their papers. She was so aggravated about the extra reading and the load of papers she faced over the *holiday* weekend, as well as the discomfort of schlepping it all out to the lot, that she didn't even notice the dark green convertible parked in the lot. There weren't that many cars left, since most of the teachers believed in leaving the premises right after the students did. *Right after?* She snorted. *They take off like their asses are on fire. Especially on a Friday, and even more so on a three-day week-end. Oh well, I'm always the last to leave. At least there's no one around to watch me, in case I drop anything or fall over.*

Determined not to drop the box before she got it to her truck, she concentrated on reaching for her keys while juggl-ing the shoulder bag and her purse. Horrified, she felt herself tripping over the concrete block that marked the end of the parking space next to hers. Heroically saving the box by throwing it into the back of her truck and grabbing the end of it to save herself from falling, she was dismayed to notice out of the corner of her eye that a man was getting out of the car parked close to hers. *He's probably getting a real chuckle out of watching me. Never even giving a thought to offering to help.*

She was so aggravated that her situation was being ob-served that she felt even more stubbornly determined not to need help. *Who the hell does he think he is?* She hit the button on her fob to open the cab door, only turning when she heard him speak.

"Melanie?"

That voice sounds familiar. She turned to see who knew her name, and almost stopped breathing. "Marcus?" She gaped at him in disbelief. *Yes. Those same familiar dark eyes. The glasses pretty much the same. The hair still closely cropped — no 'fro for this guy — he prefers his hair as short as possible. But those shoulders? Abs, visible under his tight polo shirt, since his jacket is open? Those big, muscular arms?*

She felt herself beginning to breathe even more heavily than she had been from the exertion. Warmth was starting to spread upwards and outwards, from a tiny spot in her jeans. Her knees were beginning to feel weak. In defense, she went on the offensive immediately. "Marcus, what the hell are you doing up here?"

He smiled. "Would you believe I was in the neighborhood, and thought I'd look up an old friend?"

She just stared at him. "No."

He shrugged. "Well, okay, I was in the state. I was at a conference up in Madison. I presented a paper yesterday. The business part of the event was over by noon today. I figured that it was a perfect day for a drive in the country — top down, tunes to blast. So here I am."

"You don't like being *in the country*. And Madison is a four-hour drive from here. So that's not *in the neighborhood*."

He smiled and patted the fender of his car. "No, more like two-and-a-half hours from here. But then I did have to stop for gas once."

She glanced behind him, forcing herself to tear her focus off of him long enough to look at the car he was patting. "Is that your car? Wow!"

He smiled. "Yeah, there are a few benefits to life in the big city. The big bucks let me buy a few trinkets to make my existence more bearable, even if I can't go out to look at trees and feel the grass under my feet."

She rolled her eyes. "Yeah, right. I can't remember the last time I went for a walk in the woods — or even just took a break from my homework." She gestured at the full box of files she had tossed into the back of her truck.

He studied her face.

She almost squirmed under the intensity of his stare.

"Well then, why don't you let me take you out to dinner? To try to repay you for a little of the food that you used to feed me, back when you were the only one who cared if I ate or not. Surely there must be at least one or two steak places up in this God-forsaken cow-town. I probably owe you at least a hundred dinners."

She gradually became aware that he was waiting for an answer. She was busy staring at his parts again and imagining how different the rest of him that she couldn't see must look now. *Oooh! Big shoulders — big arms — tight abs — oh my God! How long has it been for me?* Suddenly her brain flashed alarm bells in her head. "Is your divorce final yet?"

"No. But the papers are working their way through the legal system. It's only a matter of time. Besides, it's just dinner."

"Just dinner, huh? Marcus, it was never *just dinner* with us."

He moved a little bit closer to her, still studying her face.

She could feel her body stiffen as he approached her. Her breathing almost imperceptibly sped up. And she felt her face flush, aware the crimson color betrayed her thoughts to him, as it had so many times in the past.

He spoke softly. "You're looking good, Melanie. I had *almost* forgotten just how beautiful you are."

"You're looking good, too, Marcus." She shook her head to cover up her reaction to looking closely at him. She was overcome with an almost physical ache for him. She tried for a flippant attitude. "I almost didn't recognize you. You're so pumped up. I didn't realize that cardiology was such a physically-demanding job."

His lips twitched in amusement as he reached out a hand to grasp hers. "I'm not a poor under-nourished boy anymore, Melanie. I'm a full-grown man."

She tried to recover from the tingle generated by his warm hand on hers. Long-buried memories crowded in to overwhelm her. "I can see that." *And wow! What a man you've grown into.* She felt herself blushing again, sure that he could read her mind. She'd never been able to hide her lust from him, of all men.

"I may be full-grown, but I'm still always hungry, Melanie. It's really *just* dinner I'm asking you out for. Let me buy you some food, and we can talk about old times. Both of us can reminisce and relax, okay?"

She looked up at him, trying to read his expression. *Am I going to be able to tell him No later? All I can think of now is how much I want to throw him onto the hood of his car and jump on him. God help me! What the hell do I say?*

She glanced at his car, then back at him. "Can I drive your car to the restaurant?"

He smiled in surprise. "Yeah. But only on the way there. Once we have a few drinks, I have to drive back, since it's my insurance. Okay?"

"I don't drink nearly as much as I used to, you know."

"Neither do I, honey. But no one has *ever* driven my car except me. So be glad I'm letting you do more than just sit in the seat and smell it."

"Don't call me *honey*," she reminded him wearily. "You know I hate that."

"Okay — sugar." He smiled mischievously.

She stuck her tongue out at him, pleased by the hungry look that flashed across his face. "You'll have to follow me to my place, so I can leave my truck there. I'd get towed if I left it here in the school lot too late. I can change into something dressier for dinner, and you can call and make the reservations."

His eyebrows rose up in shock "Do you even need reservations up here?"

"Sure! You can call with phones and everything. And I'll put on my best gingham frock, then we can go to the hoe-down afterwards — you stuck-up, big-city snob!"

"Hey, I was only kidding. Just find me a place I can have a good steak, and I'll be happy."

"Even if it doesn't cost you an arm and a leg? How will you know it's good if the bill isn't big enough?"

He gave her a long look, long enough to make her blush again, before he answered in a low tone. "I'll know it's good, because I'll be satisfied afterwards, won't I?"

"Stop it, Marcus!"

"Stop what?"

"Just get in your fucking car and follow me."

He nodded, turning to get into his car.

She got into her truck and started to drive, trying not to think about how horny she felt, and how hot he looked — and how long it had been for her. *How the hell am I going to be able to resist him later, after a few drinks, when it took all I had to not jump him back there?* She glanced at the rear-view mirror to see Marcus right behind her.

Get a hold of yourself, Melanie! He's a married man, and you're a single teacher in a town of Moral Majority folks. Even a hint of scandal is too much. Now think of a place to take him for dinner that isn't right in town, but not so far off that he will think I'm trying to hide.

Marcus was having his own trouble keeping his mind on the road. Visions of their shared past kept imposing themselves on his brain, making it almost impossible to focus on driving. All of the blood in his body was concentrating itself in the part of him that had missed her the most.

CHAPTER FOUR: DINNER FOR TWO

They drove out of the parking lot, with Marcus following her closely. When they stopped at the light before the highway, Melanie waved for him to pull up next to her.

She rolled down the passenger window on her truck and yelled, "We have to go a few miles on the highway. Stay close. I'll try not to lose you."

Marcus snorted, pointing at her truck. "Lose me? In that? I don't think so!"

"Asshole!" Melanie mouthed at him, as she rolled her window back up. Rising to the challenge, Melanie shifted into first gear before the light changed. Once it did, she was off and running.

Marcus let her get ahead of him, then followed her as closely as he dared.

"Get any closer and you can just ride in my goddamned trunk." Melanie muttered, as the jag in the Jaguar stuck to her bumper like glue. Whenever she sped up, so did he. When she slowed down, due to traffic, he almost drove right into her.

The ride to her exit took almost no time at all, since they mostly did eighty miles an hour. Once they turned off the by-pass, Marcus pulled up next to her again, grinning.

Melanie stuck her tongue out at him. She drove on, fully aware that he had no idea where she lived. Since she had a four-wheel-drive truck, she could drive him right through a corn field if she wanted to, and he'd be forced to follow. The idea of watching as his alignment was shot to hell amused her so much that she almost turned off the road, just to see what he would do. But her better nature forced her to just drive home. So a few minutes after they got off of the highway, they turned down the side street that led to a newer development where her quad home was. She pulled into the driveway and parked.

Marcus pulled up behind her and parked, blocking the sidewalk.

"Hey, that's illegal you know." She pointed at his car, blocking part of the sidewalk.

"People walk out here?" He pretended to be surprised. "I thought they got used to having to drive everywhere, since they're out in the middle of fucking nowhere!"

"Ha ha. Better we should walk around out here in the fresh air than back where you live, breathing in big city pollution day and night."

"Yeah," he countered. "Since I moved out of DeKalb, I've really missed the smell of cow-shit in the morning. But then, when enough big dogs have been by, I find I don't really miss the cows. Shit is shit, after all. Plus I don't have to drive a million miles to find a good restaurant."

"We're not going that far." She struggled with the boxes of papers and the other teacher paraphernalia. "Don't bother offering to help. Not that you're big and strong, or anything."

"Hey, I don't want to be accused of insinuating that you can't do it by yourself." His lips twitched in amusement. "You did a pretty good job back at the school, so I figured you had it under control."

"Well, here." She gasped, pushing the heavy box into his arms, then grabbing everything else she needed. She struggled to hold her keys to open the door while juggling the other stuff. "I don't mind your offering to help, as long as we are all clear that I *could* do it myself, I just choose not to."

"No problem." He stood still, amazed.

"What?" She turned back toward him. "Are you suddenly a vampire or something? Do I have to formally invite you in?"

"No," he answered slowly. "I was just thinking how long it's been since I laughed at anything — or felt this relaxed talking to anyone."

Tossing her stuff onto a nearby counter, she turned to face him, motioning for him to put the box down. "You need to get out more."

"Maybe it's the company I've been keeping." He had to force himself to look up and into her eyes instead of where his attention had wandered. The exertion of carrying all her gear had made her sweat, and her now disheveled shirt was hanging open, her cleavage clearly visible to him. The rounded tops of her breasts were heaving with her heavy breathing. "I'll bet the boys in the class don't have any problems paying close attention to you, do they?"

"Oh!" She gasped, apparently realizing what he meant. Hurriedly straightening up her shirt, she abruptly changed the subject. "You've got yourself booked into a motel room, right? I mean, you're not expecting to stay here, right?"

"Yeah, I do. I checked in before I Googled your school, to get directions. Though I probably could have just driven to the big dot on the map that is your town, then wandered around looking for the sign that pointed out the way to the one high school around here. But yeah, I have a place to stay for the night. You're not tossing me out already, before dinner?" He opened his eyes wide in mock horror.

"No. I just wanted to be sure that we're both on the same page here, okay?" She spoke quickly and nervously. "I mean, I asked you not to come up to see me until your divorce was final, then you show up here and say it's not — not quite final, but close. That's not really good enough for the gossips in town, so it can't be good enough for me either. You understand, right?"

"It's okay, honey." He smiled when she flinched. "Really, I just want to go to dinner with you — to talk, reminisce, and have a few laughs. I always enjoyed your company more than anyone else I knew, even when we weren't in bed." His attempt to make her relax only made her blush. He rejoiced, realizing that he only had to refer to what they had done to make her react as if he was suggesting they reenact it.

She rummaged around in the drawers of a big desk covered with folders. When she found the phone book, she tossed it at him. "It's called Nick's Char-House." She checked her watch. "It's after five already? I need to change, and it'll take about forty-five minutes to get there. Make the reservations for six-thirty."

"Whose name do I put it under? Yours or mine?"

"Why?"

"Well, I don't want there to be any traceable proof that you were out with me." His smile was tentative. "What's worse? Under your name, and they will wonder who the hell is making the call? Or under my name, and maybe hope there won't be anyone there who recognizes you?" The look he gave her was casual, but he hoped she'd realize he was anxious to please her and trying to figure out how.

"Put it under your name, I guess. But for your information, mister, at least two of my students work there as waitresses. If I wanted to take you somewhere that no one would recognize me, we'd have to drive damn near back to Madison So no smart-ass shit from you anymore, please!" She flounced into the next room and slammed the door.

He called after her. "Aren't you going to give me a tour?"

"No," she yelled from what he assumed was the bedroom. "It's not big enough to need a tour. Bathroom's next to the kitchen — door's open. You're in the living room. The dining area is in between, or in the kitchen. That's it. There's your tour. Now make yourself useful and make those reservations."

He looked around at the raised counter between the kitchen and living room with three padded barroom chairs. He pulled out the closest chair and took out his phone to make the call. Out of habit, he asked if there was a dress code.

There was an amused girlish giggle on the other end and he heard some gum popping. "Hey, as long as you're not naked, we'll serve you dinner."

With a smile he put down the phone. Memories came crashing back again, and he remembered how much he had always enjoyed being naked with Melanie. Even when they had a fight, which was rare, the making up always made it worth it. He hoped he wasn't going to have to fight with her tonight, to get her to agree with what they both wanted. But he'd gone a few rounds with her before. And usually considered himself the winner.

CHAPTER FIVE: MORE MARCUS MEMORIES

The fall semester after their summer together was particularly brutal in workloads for them both. Marcus found the competition to be almost unbearable as other students vied to show that they were better than the *charity case* or *ghetto-boy*, as some of them called him. While he was aware that the crushing load of work they all had to face was partly responsible, he resented being made to feel that he was second best in any way. Especially when he was scoring the highest grades in the class often enough to draw attention to himself.

For her part, Melanie was doing so much writing that she didn't have the time or the energy left to hang out in the bars as often as she used to do. More and more, she told Marcus, she relied on knowing that she would see him on Tuesdays and Saturdays for her sexual pleasures. She never mentioned the words *falling in love*, but Marcus hoped she felt the same way he did, because for him, the falling had come a long time ago.

On the odd occasion that she did manage to get out to the bars to party without him, she told him she usually felt too guilty to bring anyone home with her. But the lure of the unknown was hard to ignore, and not having denied herself anything for years, she still succumbed to her own inclinations occasionally. Not very often, but occasionally. A specific memory surfaced.

Marcus had called and angrily insisted Melanie get her roommate out for an hour so he could come over.

When he got to her apartment, he pounded on the door.

She opened it, trepidation radiating from her.

He simply glowered at her.

"Want a beer?" she asked him.

He pushed by her to stalk over to the couch, where he plopped himself down onto the one end of it, not looking at her at all. "No."

"All-righty, then. Want to tell me what's got your undies in a bunch?"

She must be trying to jolly him out of his mood, but he was having none of it. "For God's sake, why him?" he spat out savagely. "How many thousands of men are there on this fucking campus anyway? Why him?"

"Oh-kay. I'm guessing there's some reason why you're so pissed at me?"

"I beat him on the last couple of tests. He's been trying to shove in my face how fucking superior he is to me, and I've beaten him on all the tests. So he had to find a weak spot to use to get at me—and you had to let him?" His tone was one of utter betrayal.

"Who?"

"Fucking *Bill-the-dildo!*" he yelled at her. "The white boy who's pissed that I have more intelligence in my dick than he does in his whole body!"

She wrinkled her brow for a moment. "You mean William? Blond, about six feet tall, looks like a football-player? Only slightly more intelligent-looking?"

"Yes! That's the asshole! Why him? Why?"

She got up and got herself a beer, opened it, then took a drink before she answered, defensively, standing in front of him. "Why not? He looked cute. He bought me a couple of drinks. He told me this story about not getting laid very often because everyone was too intimidated by his looks, figuring that he had no trouble with women. He said he was a shy guy. How the hell was I supposed to know that he knew you?"

"He's a goddamned med student! Didn't you even learn that much before you dragged him up to your bed?" He snarled at her, not even trying to hide his disgust.

"No," she replied coolly. "I usually don't bother to ask. It's so cliché to ask *What's your major?* Why should I care what he's studying? I'm not inviting him up here to do homework together."

"Why do I bother?" His voice was resigned as he got up and brushed past her, heading for the door.

"Marcus! You come back here! What the fuck? You come in here and lay this shit at my door, now you're gonna just get up and leave? I don't think so! Get back here and tell me what this is all about."

"You," he said wearily. "This is all about you."

"How?"

Slowly he trudged back to the couch and sat as far away from where she had perched as was possible. He talked slowly, painfully. "*Bill the dildo* strutted into class today as if he owned the place. He immediately started talking to his buddies about the great lay he had last night. He said he didn't think he'd enjoy it so much, since the woman was kind of a slut. He heard that she's sampled so many men on campus that he figured she wouldn't have any muscle tone left — where it counts. But he just had to do her because he was wondering what kind of woman she really was — since he'd heard that she was the favorite of someone in the class. Then they all laughed and turned to look at me. *So, how was she?* another guy asked, and good ol' Bill launched into a very graphic description of how the night went, how amazing you were, complete with sound effects, to the great amusement of everyone around him." Marcus stopped, nearly overcome again with pain.

"So," she asked quietly. "What happened next?"

"Nothing. I got up and left the room. What the hell else was I supposed to do? He obviously used you to get at me—and it worked. I wanted to punch him out, but I couldn't take the chance of being suspended or dropped from the program. So I just left. And I didn't even have any money to get drunk on. So I just walked around and tried to deal with my anger. But I can't. I just can't. And now I don't know what the hell I'm going to do, since I need to pass that class to finish the program. It's too late to drop it. There won't be time to take it next semester. I'm so screwed." He sighed and leaned forward, putting his head into his hands dejectedly.

Melanie got up and paced the room, muttering to herself. Eventually she chugged the last of her beer. She strode to the fridge and took out two new bottles and screwed the covers off of both. She walked over to where Marcus sat, unmoving. She dropped to her knees and put the bottles on the table as she assumed the pose of a supplicant. "If I say I'm sorry—and beg you—will you forgive me for not asking what his major was? Or if he knew you? Or if he was trying to use me to hurt the man I love?"

Slowly Marcus looked up and into her eyes. "Do you really? Love me, I mean."

She shifted nervously, but still met his eyes. "Of course I do, you silly man."

"Then why do you still pick up other men in the bars?"

She shrugged elaborately. "Habit? I don't know. Maybe being too tied to you scares me. So I do it as an act of defiance, to show you that you don't own me."

He took her face in both of his hands, forcing her to look up and into his eyes. "What are you afraid of? You've owned me since the first time you touched me. I get horny, I think of you. I want to talk to someone who understands, I think of you. I want to celebrate—or commiserate with someone, I think of you. I don't want anyone else—only you. How could you hurt me like this?"

Tears filled her eyes. "I didn't mean to hurt you. I didn't really think of you at all. I guess I figured that you'd never find out about it, so it didn't matter. How was I to know that he was doing it to hurt you? He used me like a pawn. And you know what the worst part is?" Dramatically, she paused. "He was no goddamned good in bed! I didn't even get to enjoy it, and it was already over. And now I find that he got more enjoyment in the retelling and embellishing than in the doing. Because I sure don't remember doing any noise making. I certainly didn't moan or scream. Hell, I wasn't even sure he was doing anything at all, until he started to breathe really heavy."

Marcus leaned forward dejectedly. "I've tried to be an understanding lover, but I'm sorry, Melanie. I don't think I can do this anymore."

"Do what?"

"I can't go on sharing you with any Tom, Dick, or Harry that you pick up for the night. I don't want to make you choose. So maybe I should just leave now."

"Why?" Her voice was shrill with fear. "Don't you want me anymore?"

Marcus moved closer before he grabbed both sides of her face with his hands, forcing her to look deeply into his eyes. "I will *always* want you. I told you, you marked my soul the first time you touched me. But I can't share you anymore. It's not enough for me to be *one of your men* anymore. I still don't have any more time to spend with you. But knowing that you are with other guys is becoming more torture than I can take. I can't think about the work I have to do, because I'm wondering who you're with, and if you are enjoying him more than you enjoy me. This thing with Bill is just the last straw—

but it's been coming on for a while now. I want you to belong to *just me*, but I feel like a shit because you never offered to do that. I can't ask you to marry me because you've told me you never want to get married. I can't ask you to not see other men because that's not part of our arrangement. But I can't keep on like this. And I don't know what the hell to do about it."

He sighed heavily. Responding to the desolate look on her face, he bent his face to kiss her—to kiss away any pain he was causing her. The next instant they were tearing each other's clothes off and frantically grabbing and clutching at each other, kissing, biting, squeezing, breathing heavily, hearts pounding with passion not to be denied. Once they were done stripping each other, he pulled her up to straddle his lap, and she rubbed her hard nipples against his chest, then licked and bit him, claiming him for herself.

"You see?" He groaned. "You always do that to me. I can't even think about another woman. There's only you for me." He spread her legs and pushed into her, without checking to see if she was wet enough to take him. It was a tight fit, but he was determined.

It only took a few thrusts before she threw her head back, screaming out an orgasm.

Triumphant, Marcus ploughed repeatedly into her, all the while muttering. "See? You're *my* girl! You belong to *me*! I make you scream! *I* make you come! *You're mine!*"

Another wave of pleasure hit her—she screamed again. That last scream did it, and Marcus slammed himself into her so hard he knew there would be bruises on both of them. He howled as his orgasm gave him the release he needed—of his passion, his anger, and his frustration. Everything else left him then. The only emotion he felt, as always when he held her in his arms afterwards, was love. He would die to protect this woman. *My woman.*

Gradually Melanie's breathing slowed and her heartbeat

returned to normal. Suddenly she jerked her head up to glare into Marcus' eyes. "Hopefully I'm far enough into my cycle that I won't get pregnant from that!"

"Baby, I don't even care anymore." Marcus panted as he spoke.

"But I do!" She sounded angry.

The sound of a key in the lock made them both start, then jump up, trying to race into her room before her roommate opened the door. Marcus was taller and quicker. Melanie tripped over the coffee table and fell onto all fours as her roommate walked in, talking and looking backwards at the guy she was leading into the apartment.

"Jesus, you guys!" she yelled, when the guy's eyes widened and his lips twitched in amusement. "Get a room! Get *into* a room! It's not fucking Tuesday! Can't I ever get laid around here?"

"Ooops! Sorry!" Melanie pushed herself upright and staggered, limping, picking up clothes along the way, holding them in front of her, heading in the direction of her room. "We'll be out of the way in no time! Marcus, let's go get some food."

Laughing, Marcus reached over to help her walk, and they retired to her room to put on the clothes they had torn off and thrown all around the living room. He grabbed the beers once they were dressed and on their way out of the apartment. They finished them as they walked to their favorite Mexican restaurant.

They ate more tacos than were healthy for people to eat in one night, especially people who planned to be intimate with each other. Afterward they walked back to the bar that they had met in, to talk over their situation.

"Honestly, Melanie," Marcus said as she paid for their beers. "Someday I will be the man and pay for everything you need. I don't know just when that will be, but someday."

"Marcus, if I cared, I would have dumped you a long time ago." She shrugged. "We each bring what we have to this relationship, and we each get our jollies from it. I'm not keeping score."

He sighed. "It's just that the man is supposed to pay, at least some of the time. I have nothing to offer to you except my big hard cock."

She smiled at him and reached over to rub him through his jeans. "No, Marcus, you give *yourself* to me. That's really all I want from you. You're right, you know —" she snapped her fingers in his face, causing him to focus on her instead of on how her rubbing was making him feel.

He shook his head and smiled, giving her his full attention.

"When you said that there's more to *us* than being good in bed together. No matter how good that is, you can't live in bed. Even when we're not fucking, I still like to be around you. We can talk — laugh — I enjoy just being with you. You're one of my best friends. And considering most of the rest of them are women, and the few that *are* men I don't sleep with, you're a really special person in my life. So don't you go feeling like you're just taking and not giving, okay?"

"So, what are we going to do about us?" He didn't want to bring up their recent argument but was unwilling to just pretend it hadn't happened. He needed resolution.

She sighed heavily. "So what you *are* asking me to do is to give up other men entirely, right? No more seducing my professor, then both of his sons, in my own private version of *A Family Affair*? No more walking into the bar, exhilarated by the hunt, not knowing just who I would pick up, but knowing that no matter who I chose, he'd be mine that night?"

"Would that really be so hard?" He pulled her hand up off of his erection and held it, looking into her eyes. "What would it take? Another night of the week, so you could have three nights of energetic fucking? Four nights?" He tried to show her his love with his eyes.

"Do you really mean to say that you would sacrifice your degree, just to have me to yourself?"

When he looked confused, she relented. "No, I don't want you to do that, and neither do you." She looked away briefly, before turning back to him. "No, Marcus, I'll voluntarily give up picking up other men in bars as long as I can have you reliably, twice a week. If you get a not-so-busy week and can squeeze in another night or two, then that's just wonderful. But this semester is almost over, and I have tons of work to do before it ends. And remember, I'll be student-teaching next semester, so I won't have much time to spare either. We'll both be in the same boat. I guess I might as well get used to being monogamous now."

He leaned over to kiss her deeply, soul-searchingly, tasting her capitulation, along with the sweet victory of having won what he had been wanting from her for such a very long time. "You won't be sorry, baby," he whispered. "I'll do my best to keep you so satisfied that you won't even miss me on the nights I'm not there. You'll be too busy recovering for the next time."

She leaned into his mouth again, forcing his lips to open, then pushing her tongue into his, as if aware for the first time that she was tasting his love. "But what are we going to do now? My roomie's getting laid in the apartment. Where can we go?"

Half an hour later she waited, leaning on the wall next to his dorm room door.

He was reminding his roommate about the few times he had slept out in the commons area when the girl from back home had been up for a visit. "Think of this as the one and only time I have ever asked for payback time. So vacate."

Soon the door was thrown open and his roommate

staggered out, buried under books, papers, and a blanket. After a brief nod to Melanie for a greeting, he made his way down the hall to the commons area for the night.

They stripped quickly, tearing at their clothes in urgency. Marcus pushed her to bend over the desk against the wall. He got onto his knees behind her to reach up and separate her folds with his fingers. He licked and lapped at her, then blew cool air onto the wetness, making her. Then he dove into her with his tongue, first poking it into her, lapping at her juices like a cat with cream, before rasping his tongue from front to back. She moaned when he licked around the rim of her anus, then pushed his way into that part of her also, as if to claim what he hadn't yet taken.

Melanie panted, her breathing coming quicker and quicker.

Marcus licked back up to her clit and sucked on it, while he poked two fingers into her, one into each hole.

Melanie screamed as she came, sobbing out his name while she twitched repeatedly on his fingers.

Marcus rose and fumbled for a condom from his pants pocket. Melanie was still standing bent over from the waist, leaning on the desk and shaking with each breath. He spread her legs into a V shape and reached down to find her still dripping fluids, still quivering from his touch. He bent his legs slightly, since she was shorter than he was, then rammed his way into her body with one forceful thrust.

She was wet and tight and more than ready for him. He reached around to pull on her nipples as they moved, her breasts bouncing against his desk when he pushed forward. Then he reached one hand further down and tickled her clit while he pulled on a nipple, still pulling himself almost all the way out to ram himself back into her, over and over again. When the pressure began to build again and he knew he was losing the battle to control himself for much longer, he grabbed both of her hips to hold her still, riding her forcefully, neither of them caring that the imprint of his fingers would be on her skin for weeks.

Melanie shrieked at the same time that Marcus howled, both of them incoherent in their passion. Orgasms rippled through them both, causing spasms that were kinetic—one would spasm, causing the other to experience another ripple of orgasm, which would create a spasm, that made the other one ripple into more orgasms.

When Marcus finally collapsed, he crushed Melanie into the desk. They lay panting and gasping, waiting for their heartbeats to slow down enough for thought to be possible.

Suddenly there was the sound of loud applause from the next room, as male voices whooped and hollered in exaggerated excitement, pounding on the wall next to Melanie's head.

"You da man!"

"Show her who's boss!"

"Who's your daddy now, bitch?"

"Give it to her good!"

Marcus was momentarily horrified when he felt Melanie shaking beneath him, afraid that she was embarrassed to tears. He raised himself up and asked tentatively, "Are you all right, honey?"

Melanie pushed herself up off the desk and turned, and he saw that she was laughing. "Haven't you ever had a woman in here?"

He shook his head, smiling. "You would know, baby. You're the only woman for me."

She shook her head slowly, in wonder. "Now *that* I don't understand. But I'm willing to give it a try." She suddenly looked serious. "I don't want to lose you, Marcus. You mean too much to me."

They smiled before kissing gently yet passionately, hands traveling to favorite places to fondle with familiar touches.

Since Marcus didn't have anything to drink in his room, he snuck out into the hallway to fill a water bottle, then returned to find Melanie had stretched out on the bottom bunk, which he had told her was his bed. He clicked off the light before joining her. Despite it being a tight squeeze, they settled comfortably into each other's arms.

"I'm not sure if I can sleep like this all night, though," Melanie said after a while, during which time they had run their hands over each other possessively. "I'll get a crick in my neck from having it bent up to rest on your shoulder."

They separated then, lying side-by-side on the small, twin bed. They lay in silence for a while before Marcus spoke softly. "Melanie? Are you asleep?"

"Almost. Why?"

"Did you really sleep with a professor and both of his sons?"

There was a snort of laughter. "Do you really want to know the answer to that?"

"I—I guess not. Forget it."

Melanie turned to lean on his chest. "Marcus, look at me."

He could barely make out her face in the moonlight streaming in through the window.

"It was the second semester of my first year here. I was sowing a whole lotta wild oats, what with feeling free of the restraints of living in my parents' house and being able to stay out all night if I wanted to. I hadn't met you yet. It was years ago. There's no reason for you to be jealous of something that happened before I met you."

Marcus pulled her face down to kiss her possessively.

With a sigh she snuggled back into his arms.

"I know that. I also know that there's a whole lot of men I could be jealous of, but hunting them down one by one wouldn't change anything. It's just that I love you so much. I want you to belong only to me."

Melanie smiled so broadly with her face against his chest that Marcus felt her dimples deepen. "Well, I do now, mister. So you'd better be eating your *Wheaties* to keep your strength up. You're gonna have to work really hard to keep me happy, since I've never been able to get everything I want from just one man."

Marcus sighed with contentment.

"Marcus?"

"What?"

"Think you're up for it?"

"Again? Now?"

"No, silly man. I mean, for the long-term?"

"I'll give it my best shot."

Melanie nodded, smiling again. "Good-night, lover."

Marcus was the one to smile now. "Good-night, ho—"

He smiled even more broadly when she slapped him gently on the arm. Then she snuggled back into his side, and soon they were both asleep.

When the alarm went off at six am, Melanie hit her head on the top bed as she sat up. She jumped out of bed to get ready to leave.

Marcus helped her to find all of her clothes and kissed her deeply and thoroughly. "Today is Friday. I've got too much work to make-up, since I've been too upset to get anything done. But Saturday night looks good. Should I meet you in the bar?" He was reluctant to let her go without an assurance of the next time.

"You know, maybe in light of our new relationship, I'll try to make you dinner. How's that sound?" She had a challenge in her voice.

"I don't know." He sounded skeptical. "I thought you didn't know how to cook."

"I don't. But how hard can it be to follow a recipe?"

"Okay. I guess as long as you don't poison me too much."

"Hey! I'll be eating the same shit, you know. Just be at my place about seven, and I'll figure out what we're going to be eating. I mean, besides each other." She snickered before she leaned into him, pulling his head down for a final kiss, pressing herself against him, rubbing herself on him. She stroked him once, twice — then she left the room.

Marcus stood in his doorway and watched her walk down the hall, once again admiring how fine her ass looked as she rolled her hips. He rejoiced that he had finally been able to convince her to give up other men for him. He didn't know for how long, or even *if* that would last, but he had won one round in the battle to keep her for himself. Almost a year of trying, and he finally had what he wanted. *No, I won't really have what I want until I know for a fact that she's mine. Once I get her to marry me, then I can relax.* He thought about that for a moment. *Ah, Hell, who am I kidding? I'm gonna have to work my whole life to keep that woman in line! But someday that fine ass of hers is going to belong to me.* With that thought making him smile, he went down the hall to wake up his roommate.

CHAPTER SIX: MELANIE'S MEMORIES

Marcus seemed lost in his memories when Melanie opened the door. She stood admiring the man from her past, who had intruded into her present. She was struck by just how virile he looked — strong, masculine — *finished*, as opposed to the skinny boy she had fallen so madly in love with so many years ago. His shoulders had broadened, his waist was defined, but he still had the sexiest ass she had ever seen on a man, sitting on top of the longest legs. His hair was still short, his face had grown quite a few lines on it. Would his eyes still burn with desire when he looked at her?

This man had once been hers and she had left him. He had asked her to marry him and she had told him *No*. Why? She told herself it was because of what his mother had said. Mama Jones was afraid of him being too distracted by her to do what he had to do to succeed. He had more schooling to get through, as well as his residency. He had a long, hard road still ahead of him. She was afraid that Melanie would keep him from achieving his life's goal of becoming a cardiologist. His mom had asked Melanie to give him a chance to be by himself, to impress the world, to become what he had always wanted to be. But to be honest, at least with herself, it wasn't just about what his mother had said.

Marcus had transferred to the University of Chicago Medical School to do his final years of specialty training, learning new ways to provide cardiac care. He would then have to do his residency there also. He had to be in the middle of a big city in order to achieve his lifetime career goals. And Melanie could not face living in such a huge metropolitan area. Born and raised in a small town in northern Illinois, with half of her friends and relatives dairy farmers, she quaked inwardly whenever she was forced to head out of her comfort zone into any city that big. He wanted her to live with him in down-town Chicago, in the heart of a neighborhood that gave her nightmares just thinking about it.

She had gone with him just that once to meet his family and was shocked by the gritty reality of their lives. The roaches and rats, the dingy peeling paint on the walls, the smell of urine and unwashed bodies in the elevators and the hall-way—everything that he was trying to escape was still a part of where he would have to live while he worked eighty hour weeks to make a name for himself. She told him honestly that she couldn't live like that.

She wanted to teach English, but not in a high school where she had absolutely nothing in common with the students—where the kids would treat her like the *sheltered white bread* that she was. Absolute truth was that she was afraid of all of it—the city, the crowds, the reality that she would be alone much of the time without him there to make her feel better—the feeling that she would be a fish out of water. And she was even afraid of him. The commitment they had made to each other was not meant to last a lifetime. She hadn't meant it to. When she realized that he did, she took a job offer in upper Wisconsin, near where she had some family. She told him af-ter the graduation ceremonies were all over with, and every-one was leaving to start their new lives.

His eyes hadn't been burning with desire then. They were filled with tears he refused to shed. He didn't want to hear any explanations about different life-styles, or growing in dif-ferent directions, or anything else that she had rehearsed to tell him, to soften the fact that she was leaving him.

His last words haunted her still. "You're *my* woman,

Melanie. You marked my soul—I hope to hell I've marked yours. Years from now you'll burn for *me*, wanting me in your bed, but you'll know you left me. No man will ever satisfy you the way I do. We both know the truth of that." Then he had turned and walked away from her.

She cried for the next two days, because what she was afraid of, most of all, was that he was right.

Was he? Was he right? Is that why no other man has ever been good enough for me? Pickings got mighty slim when I moved back to a small town similar to the area that I grew up in. The occasional single father asked me out, but that was a loaded gun not worth playing with. If things didn't work out, there would be speculations about my sex life that would make it impossible for me to continue teaching. Not quite as demanding as being Caesar's wife, above reproach, still I'm expected to behave in a chaste manner, and to set a good example for the kids. Yea, right! The kids who are out rutting after each other every night, while I lie in my bed burning with desires that I have to satisfy for myself.

The last time she could remember being with a man was over a year ago, when one of her best friends got married. She hooked up with one of the groomsmen, a college friend of the groom. That had been a fun weekend. But the guy ruined the memory by wanting them to move in together right away. He figured that once they had sex—admittedly good sex—but not *set-the-world-on-fire sex*—that she was going to marry him and give him lots of babies, turning into *Susie Homemaker*, after she quit her *little job*, since he was making piles of money in car sales commissions.

She laughed at him, at his quaint notions of her place in life. His male ego was offended enough for him to call her a few choice names, then walk out on her, leaving a bad taste in her mouth that made her want to give up men entirely.

Once again, she had thrown herself wholeheartedly into her work. She went back to staying up late to grade papers, designing lesson plans tailor-made to reach even the most unresponsive students. She went in early, stayed late, coached the speech team, helped with the school newspaper, headed the literary magazine committee, and in short, lived and breathed only for her students. She had earned tenure years earlier, and now got her only satisfaction from the achievements of her students.

Occasionally one of the seniors, or even an ex-student on break, egged on by his friends or his massive ego, would try to hit on her. She was still thin, still in good shape, and still looked younger than her thirty-two years. *Hell, actresses my age routinely play high school students.*

But even without the threat of statutory rape charges, she quailed with embarrassment at the idea that she would need to stoop to having sex with former students, just to get laid. *Is there anything more pitiful than a horny older woman willing to put up with the ineptness of youth, just to get some? Hell, I didn't really like high school boys when I was in high school. At that time I was busy seducing their older brothers, or their dads – even my single teachers. The thought of having to tell them where to touch me, and for how long, just seems like such a lot of work, for so little reward. And since I spend my days teaching young minds, do I really want to do that on my off-time too? Sure there would be the whole energy thing – but where would be the conversation? The connection? The sex might be good, but what would we talk about afterwards? "Hey, how about that C I gave you in English class, eh?" No thank-you.*

So the years had passed, going faster all the time. She had been teaching in this town for ten years, and she wondered if she was ever going to experience anything like the love she'd had all those years ago. Was she happy with her life? Sometimes. Yet sometimes she wished with all her heart that she hadn't been such a coward, and had taken a chance and married the only man she had ever allowed to touch her emotions, as well as her body.

When his name had popped up on her Facebook page, her

heart had skipped a few beats, and her panties had immediately pooled with desire. Just thinking about him again made her so hot she had to satisfy herself before she could sleep that night. When he told her he was married, she almost cried. Fortunately he wasn't there in person to watch her reaction. "Separated, working on getting a divorce," he told her. "The soon-to-be-ex wants more money, more stuff, a pound of flesh and then some. Once she feels she has taken me for everything she wants, she'll sign the damn papers."

She told him not to come up to visit her until the divorce was final, because she didn't trust herself not to jump his bones the minute she saw him. Not only was she so horny she could cry from the sheer ache of loneliness, but memories of what they had done with each other so many times burned through her, making her pain even more intense. She didn't trust herself any more than she trusted him, so she didn't want him to visit.

He also told her he was probably being followed by a private detective, hoping to catch him *in flagrant delecto* — she believed him. And she also believed that if she got named in court in a divorce suit as *the other woman*, even though far away in downtown Chicago, it would have repercussions in her small-town world that she was afraid to face. So fear was once again fighting with desire, in her soul. *Which will win? That's what we're going to find out tonight over dinner, right?*

Resolutely, she walked into the room.

He stood up, his fevered gaze taking in her flimsy black dress that managed to reveal more than it covered.

Luckily I spend time at the school gym, so I'm only slightly curvier than I was in college. I think I look good for my age. He looks great!

He had changed clothes also, from his jeans and polo shirt to a buttoned shirt and nicer slacks. His jacket was hanging open again.

No matter. As far as we're both concerned, the best way to see the other one is naked. The bitch of it is that we both know it.

She gave him a tentative smile. "Ready?"

He held out her jacket for her to slip her arms into it. "Are you?"

"Let's do this." She held her hand out for his keys.

Wordlessly, he dropped them into her palm, looking afraid to touch her hand, as if in fear that he wouldn't be able to stop touching her.

With a last look around the room, she headed out the door.

Marcus was right behind her. He brushed against her as she turned to lock the door. There were two quick, sharp inhalations and exhalations as they both struggled to control their emotions.

She decisively locked the door and they got into his car. After extensively adjusting the seat and the mirrors, she drove them out to dinner to satisfy the one appetite they both felt safe acknowledging.

CHAPTER SEVEN: JUST DINNER?

M elanie laughed again, enjoying the feeling of power as she shifted the car into a higher gear. *Driving his car is almost as good as sex!* She snuck a quick look at Marcus' profile. *No, nothing is as good as sex with you, Dr. Marcus. But this does feel really good.*

Marcus was glad she was driving. That gave him the chance to look at her while she was looking at the road. They chatted easily about inconsequential things—whom they kept in touch with from college, who had married or divorced whom, who had kids, etc. And while they were talking, he snuck in glances at her, drinking in the sight of her. *Her new hairstyle is much shorter than it was in college, but it suits her well. It shows off her elfin features, making her look like a luscious pixie.* He tried to look lower than her face but found that the erection he was fighting got more insistent when he did. So he tried to concentrate on what she was saying to him.

The drive took less than the forty-five minutes she predicted, because she kept pushing his car to faster and faster speeds. She seemed to know how to do it, shifting gears like a pro. He wanted to make some remark about how well she handled his finely-tuned machine but realized that was much too dangerous for both of them.

Behave yourself, Marcus, he told himself firmly. *Or this dinner will be over before you even get to eat it.*

When they got to the restaurant, Melanie pulled into the lot and found a far-off spot, parking the car with a flourish. She turned to him, still flushed with excitement over how well it handled. She dropped the keys into his hand, making a point of not touching him.

When they were seated at a table by a window over-looking a pond and had a bottle of cabernet opened and two glasses poured, Marcus leaned over the table towards her. "A toast, my dear, to old friends. Sometimes the best ones are the ones you thought you had lost."

She gave him a long look, then said teasingly, "Yes, a toast to old friends. Especially the ones who finally repay their debts."

"What? You mean you're not paying tonight?"

"Sheesh! Give me a break! Judging by that car of yours, you could buy this whole fucking restaurant on your credit card. What's your limit, anyway? A million bucks?"

"Ha ha," he retorted. "I had to spend so much money on the gas to get all the way up here that I'll barely be able to afford dinner. Maybe we can order one entrée and split it?"

"Not a chance, big guy. I'm ordering my favorite, a filet, and you can order whatever you want."

"Even dead fish?" he teased.

She answered him without thinking. "Did you bring your toothbrush?"

"Why? Do you plan on kissing me tonight?"

She blushed, a bright pink that worked its way up from her breasts to her throat, to heat her face. "We'll see." She stammered her reply in a husky voice.

Fortunately the waitress returned at that moment, and ordering took their attention away from the steadily-increasing tension that was building between them. They were both grateful for the diversion, and they stuck to innocent topics and avoided innuendos throughout dinner.

Melanie was fascinated by the procedure that Marcus had developed and perfected, which had been named *The Jones Method* and was saving lives on a daily basis. She was even more impressed by how easily he wore his fame and his wealth. He definitely was not the raw unfinished boy he had been when they were in college. He was a cultured, experienced man. She realized that if she had just met him, she would be doing her best to entice him to spend the night with her. And she also realized that if she *had* just met him, she wouldn't necessarily ask him if he was married, and she might not find out the truth until after she had bedded him. So she put aside her guilt at being out with him, deciding to just enjoy their time together.

Marcus found himself feeling more relaxed than he had for years. She asked the right questions to show that she was listening and thinking about what he was saying. It was such a welcome change from his soon-to-be-ex-wife, who only wanted him to listen to her, not to engage in real conversation. He had not felt guilty at all about asking her out to dinner, and he rejoiced in the easy relationship they were able to revive as long as they both ignored the sexual tension that was simmering under the surface. He wondered how long they would be able to ignore it. As it was, he was glad they were sitting across the table from each other, so his throbbing erection, hidden under his napkin, wasn't noticeable to her.

Once the bottle of wine was gone, along with their dinner, they both ordered coffee. "No dessert, please," they both agreed.

"Wow," Marcus remarked after the waitress brought their coffees. "You people really do know how to do good steaks up here."

"Of course we do," Melanie said brightly. "Since we kill them right out back when you order. Couldn't you hear the fearful *mooing* when we both ordered steak? Thank God you didn't order the fish. It's a bitch to watch them trying to catch the right kind out of that pond out there."

"Ha ha. Okay, I deserved that. But seriously, I can't remember when I have enjoyed myself more. And I don't know what I enjoyed more—eating that great food, or the stimulating conversation with you. What more could a man ask?"

This time her blush wasn't nearly as dark, but he rejoiced to see just how easily he could get to her. Since he didn't want the night to end, he wasn't pushing too hard—yet. But Marcus was now even more determined not to spend any time in his motel room. Not when Melanie was right here with him, wearing a dress that only served to accentuate her curves—that was even now calling his attention to notice her slightly flushed breasts that rose and fell with her breathing, which sped up when she noticed him looking.

"So, Marcus," she changed the subject. "I haven't asked, but I've been dying to know. What led you to get married?"

He sighed, knowing that her curiosity was inevitable, but not wanting to spend his time with her talking about another woman. "Well, once I was an established cardiologist and had developed my technique, I found myself getting invited to fund-raisers for the hospital. Before that I had no time for a social life. I basically lived for my work. Half the time I lived at the hospital. I was on call a whole lot for years, and in a hospital that size in a city that big, there really was no point to going home, only to get called right back in before I got a chance to do more than change my clothes."

He laughed ruefully. "In fact, I developed *The Jones Method* in the first place to try to buy myself some extra sleep time."

"Those eighty-hour work-weeks you were *looking forward to* before we graduated, huh?"

"Yeah." He sighed again, remembering. "Anyway, I really dreaded those society things, since I don't really dance all that well, and making small talk with vapid, boring rich people is not really my idea of a good time. But still, everyone wanted to meet the famous Dr. Jones, so I really had no choice. I actually met a lot of my former and future patients that way. It has gotten to the point where I can only take care of the extremely wealthy ones, because I have no choice in who my patients are, and they are the only ones who can afford me."

Her eyebrows rose in surprise. "Not exactly what you had in mind back then, though, is it?"

"No." He shook his head, realizing he hadn't really thought of that before. "But anyway, at one of those dinners I met Shandra."

"Let me guess." Melanie jumped in. "She walked up to you, introduced herself, and proceeded to take charge of the conversation. She made it seem like you were the one doing the pursuing, but somehow, without your knowing how, she finagled you into asking her out. By the time you left that night you had a date with her, and she had managed to get you to kiss her."

She looked at him triumphantly. "Am I right?"

"Yeah. How did you know?"

"Because, Marcus, that's the kind of guy you are. Women take one look at you and they know they can *play you*, because you're an honest, simple kind of man, and you're putty in their hands. That bitch!"

He smiled at her again. "Are you insinuating that I'm not cool, or suave and debonair?"

"No. I'm not insinuating — I'm saying it. You aren't. You're attractive as hell, especially with this grown-up Marcus-the-man body, but you aren't in control around women."

I am around this one, he thought, *otherwise I'd have jumped you in your apartment and we'd never have made it out to dinner.* Out loud he asked, "So do you want to hear the rest of the sad saga, or not?"

She answered him with another question. "Who asked whom to get married?"

"Well, once we finally got around to what she referred to as *doing the nasty*, she started hinting around that her friends had noticed what a cute couple we made. Little remarks like that. Then she wanted to go walking around town, window-shopping."

"Yea, I'll bet! Jewelry-store windows, huh?"

He looked wounded. "Are you telling the story of my life, or am I?"

"Okay, okay, you do the telling."

"The wedding was a really big society affair. It made all of the papers, made lots of money for lots of people. Made Mama really happy to have me marrying so well, and to a Black woman also. My whole family was really impressed by hers."

"I'm sure. None of you had met BAPs before, had you?"

He shook his head. "No, I didn't even know what that stood for until I was married to a *Black American Princess* who had the most expensive tastes of anyone I've ever met. Neither one of our places were good enough. We had to move into a new penthouse. None of our furniture was good enough. We had to special-order all custom-designed new stuff. We spent money like there was no tomorrow. But since there was always plenty more coming in, it didn't matter."

"Were you happy with her?" Melanie surprised herself with the jealousy in her voice.

"For a while. At least I thought I was happy. She was, anyway. She had a famous cardiologist for a husband, and we had every possible thing she ever wanted to buy — vacations, new cars every year, opera tickets, whatever. Then she got obsessed with the idea of making full-partner in her firm. Did I mention that she's a lawyer?"

Jealousy now burned deeply, threatening to choke her, as she realized just how perfect this other woman was for him, how much better suited to the lifestyle that he had chosen. Melanie was not used to feeling poor or frumpy, but suddenly she realized that the shoe was on the other foot. Now Marcus was in a much better financial position than she was. "So what went wrong then? You two seem to have so much in common." She tried but was unsuccessful at keeping the envy out of her voice.

Marcus felt his heart skip a beat. *She's jealous! She knows I'm divorcing my wife, and still she's jealous. She does still care about me. Maybe it won't be so hard to get her to let me stay with her.* This realization made his napkin jump. He guiltily glanced at her to see if she had noticed. She was too busy looking downcast. He longed to reach across and touch her, to let her know how he felt. "I started to feel like my life was empty."

"Empty? With a demanding job that you love, and a beautiful, successful wife? What more could you want?"

You! I wanted you! He was greatly relieved that he had managed to *not* yell that out loud. He forced himself back to his narrative. "I started to think about wanting to have kids—but she didn't want any. At least not now. I started to wonder why I wasn't enjoying my surgeries so much anymore. I was still saving lives, but only for the very rich, who could have afforded anyone. The whole thing started to feel like another kind of grind. I just started to want more out of life. I tried to explain it all to Shandra, but she never understood what I was saying. She would deliberately pick a fight with me, accusing me of not knowing what the hell I wanted, and of trying to distract her, when all she was focused on was working on becoming a full partner."

He took another sip from his coffee before continuing. "So since I didn't know just what it was that was missing from my life, or how to go about getting it, she decided that she would just ignore me to get what she felt was missing from *her* life. She started staying even later at the office, and she stopped inviting me to go with her to functions at the office. I never liked going anyway, so at first I just thought she was being kind. Finally I realized that she was deliberately cutting me out of her life, bit by bit." He stopped, surprised at how relieved he was feeling for finally being able to tell her the whole story.

"Did you care?" She whispered, as if she was afraid of the answer.

"Not by then. No. I took a trip by myself. I drove up to Vermont instead of flying, since I had to attend a conference there to do a presentation. I did a lot of thinking while I was driving. I came to the realization that I wasn't really in love with my wife. I had just let her make me think that I was. We were both so busy that I didn't even take the time to think about what we were doing—I just let her direct our lives. She's not a bad woman. We're just not right for each other. Once I began to seek out a real relationship with her, involving actual give and take, she decided she'd had enough of me. I decided I'd file for divorce when I got back. But when I got back to the penthouse, I found that she had changed the locks while I was gone. And of course she had beaten me to the punch and filed already. I was served with the papers the next day. Since most of the lawyers I knew were in her practice, I had to call on my extensive list of ex-patients to find someone willing to take on her firm, and her complaints."

Marcus sighed heavily. "She's been doing stalling tactics from the start. I've never contested anything, yet when she realized that I just wanted the whole thing to be over, she decided to ask for just one more thing—then just one more thing. This has been going on for months now. If she keeps this up, the whole divorce process is going to last longer than our marriage did."

Melanie was quiet as she looked at him. Her hand reached across the table to take his hand to comfort him. But then she pulled it back quickly, as if she didn't trust herself to touch him.

Marcus leaned forward on the table, staring into her eyes. "Do you know how I figured out I wasn't in love with her?"

Her voice broke when she tried to speak. She cleared her throat, licking her lips before she answered. "How?"

"I remember what it felt like to be in love — to feel like the world was perfect, when I was with the right woman. I remembered how it used to be between *us*. That's when I knew that I had to get away from her, to maybe get a second chance to make you realize that we still belong together."

She nervously licked her lips again, unaware of how much that small movement made him crazy, made him want to lick her all over, to kiss her and never stop.

"I think we should go now, Marcus. I need some air. It's getting really warm in here."

He signaled for the check.

A band that had been setting up as they talked, started to play. Their first number was a slow, romantic song.

Once the waitress brought them the check and he handed over his credit card, he nodded at the dance floor, a question in his eyes.

She startled, then shook her head slowly.

Marcus chose not to notice. He got up, pulling her to her feet. He slid his arms around her, pulling her close so they could sway to the rhythms of the music.

The erotic heat level charged the air around them and Melanie found it difficult to breathe. Gasping, she found herself surrounded by his scent, the smell of his skin so familiar that it made her ache with desire.

He reached down her back and caressed caress the curve of her ass, pressing her against the insistent bulge in his pants. "God, you feel so right in my arms. Like you never left." He whispered into her ear, nuzzling her neck, licking her earlobe, inhaling her scent.

Memories crashed over her and she became oblivious to their surroundings. The ten years of separation disappeared. They were back to being Marcus and Melanie, *fuck-buddies,* who were both surprised to realize that they had fallen in love.

When the music stopped, it was with great difficulty that she returned her focus to the here and now. Marcus led her back to the table where he added the tip, signed the check, and put his credit card away.

She watched all his movements as if they were in slow-motion, because all she could think about was the feel of his hardness, and the smell of his skin, and she was afraid that it was already too late. With one dance he had made her come undone.

"Let's get out of here," he said.

She was too overcome to notice how unsteady his voice was.

The chill of the night air shocked her out of her reverie. They were silent as they walked back to his car.

He opened the door for her, lust sparking in his eyes as her skirt rode up while she pulled both legs into the low car.

He got into the driver's seat with difficulty. "Was there a midget driving my car?" He adjusted the seat and the mirrors to fit him again.

She tried to smile at his attempt at lightness, but the weight of her own feelings made her quiet for most of the drive back.

Marcus pulled the car into the driveway, careful to squeeze next to her truck so as not to block the sidewalk as he had done earlier. They both sat quietly as he turned the engine off. He turned to her expectantly. "Aren't you going to ask me in for a drink?" He tried, but utterly failed at sounding casual. *God, I sound so needy. Try to be cool, Marcus.*

She looked at him for a long moment before replying in a hoarse voice. "I — uh — don't think that's such a good idea."

"I promise to be good. When you tell me to leave, I will. Just one drink." He realized he was pleading, but pride wasn't even an issue anymore. He had smelled her, after watching her breasts rise and fall all night. *Damn it, woman, I held you in my arms! I have to have you tonight, or I'll go crazy!*

She studied her own folded hands in her lap.

He watched as her inner struggle raged, and he prayed that she would choose in his favor. He was afraid to touch her, for fear that she would bolt out of the car and into the house.

Finally she looked up at him. "Okay. Just one drink. Then you really have to go."

Yes! He almost came in his pants. Just the thought of being able to spend more time with her made him feel keenly the pain of riding the edge of sanity. He followed her into her apartment.

"Lock the door behind you, okay? I'll get the wine."

When he turned to look at her, she was sitting on one of the padded bar chairs, pouring them both some red wine, looking like she was on the same edge that he was on. He was desperately afraid, unsure of how to proceed without being thrown out on his ass. He wasn't sure what to say, or even if he should talk at all. So he did as he had often done way back when, and he said nothing, waiting for her to fill the silence. He sat on the chair nearest to her. He didn't have to wait long.

She sighed heavily, looking at the wine she was swirling

around her glass while she spoke to him. "Marcus, what would you do if I told you that you have to go back to your motel room? That you absolutely can't stay here?"

He felt his heart almost stop beating. He had to force himself to take a breath so he could answer her quietly. "I would only drink half of my glass of wine. I certainly would *not* try to kiss you good night. And I would drive very quickly back to that motel to take a very long, very cold shower. Why? Is that what you're telling me?"

She inhaled so slowly that it became almost a sob, as if the words themselves were causing her pain. She spoke so uncharacteristically softly that he had to lean forward to hear what she was saying to him. "You've always been an honorable man, Marcus. I wish I was an honorable woman. In fact, I wish a lot of things."

"Like what?" He was desperate for some sign as to how to please her.

"I wish I was as honorable as you are. I wish you were already divorced. I wish it had not been so fucking long since anyone was in my bed."

She stopped and took in a quavering breath before she continued. "I wish every cell in my body would stop resonating to the vibrations of your body, to your every movement. And most of all, I wish I could stop replaying in my head what it was like for us when we made love—how wonderful it was between us." She took another sip of her wine, her hands shaking with emotions she was having trouble controlling.

Marcus knew that the time had come. He leaned over the distance between them to take the glass out of her hands and put it onto the counter. He used a finger under her chin to lift her face—to force her tear-filled eyes to look at him. "I love you, Melanie. I always have, I always will. There's no one else for me. Just you." He kissed her, softly at first, then with growing strength, as his passion ignited, and they both groaned.

Later, neither of them remembered whose tongue had been the first to enter whose mouth, but it didn't matter anymore. With a low sound Melanie finally gave in, wrapping her arms around him, pulling him close to her, trying to meld their bodies into one — even with all of their clothes still on.

Now that he knew he was allowed to stay, Marcus stood up in front of her and acted on his desires. He began to undress her in the most sensuous and erotic way he could think of. Well aware that his entire future depended on seducing this woman who had forced her way into his life so long ago, he took his time with every movement. He explored her mouth before moving onto her neck, to nibble her earlobe and blow into her ear. Gently he eased off first one side then the other, of the spaghetti straps that held up her dress. He trailed his tongue along her collarbone to her shoulder as he reached around behind her to unzip the back. He eased her dress down, to finally be able to see the breasts he had been remembering from a hundred different memories. He inhaled deeply and smiled.

"You're even more beautiful than I remember," he breathed at her before he dipped his head to lick his way to her lust-hardened nipples. Licking, and then sucking each one in turn, he took pleasure in the strangled sounds she was making, as her pleasure made her twist and turn in her chair.

Her hands were in his hair, rubbing his head, holding him, moving down his back, then finally, pulling at his shirt to remove the barrier to what they both knew she wanted to do. He pulled his shirt over his head and she sucked in a breath, running her hands over his rock-hard chest and his abs. With a small cry she leaned over and licked his nipples, first one then the other; then she rubbed her face all over his chest, making small moaning noises, as she marked him again. Her tiny bites, licks and kisses drove him insane.

With a strangled moan, he breathed, "Enough." He made her rise up on the chair, standing on the footrest, as he pulled her dress all of the way down, lifting up one foot then the other, to find that the only thing she had on under her dress was a tiny lace panty, barely big enough to cover her curls.

Reverently, he pushed her to lean back on the chair and kissed her navel, then her lace, before he pulled the panty off to begin licking his way up to her paradise. He started at one ankle as he pulled that leg out of the panty, licking his way up to her knee. Then he started at the other ankle, after removing the lace blockade totally. He licked up that leg, working his way up to where she was dripping with anticipation. He toyed with her, moving his tongue from one thigh to the other, licking her all around, everywhere but where she wanted him to, flicking at her tiny engorged bud, then going back to kissing her upper thighs, sucking on them to make hickeys that would mark her as his woman. All the while, she thrashed and moaned, begging him without words to do what they both knew she wanted him to do.

Finally, unable to hold back anymore, he dove his tongue into her cleft, sweeping up to her clit and back again, repeatedly.

She came with a scream, pushing herself up and into his face, her spasms making her arch and dig her fingernails into his shoulders. "Oh my God, Marcus, yes! Yes!"

He continued with his licking as he drove her to more orgasms.

She screamed again, trembling and shaking—letting him know beyond a doubt that she still belonged to him.

When he pulled back from her, she whimpered, as if momentarily bereft of his attention.

He surged upwards to impale her on his throbbing cock, which he had freed from his pants then covered with a condom, while his tongue had been driving her mad.

Feeling him inside of her again was enough to make her scream out another orgasm, as she clenched him deep within her body. Her muscles were massaging him like a tight glove that had been specially made just for him. She matched his every movement, rolling her hips to take him deeper.

He stood before her and slid himself into her silken wet heat, then out, then back in again, deeper each time. He moaned as he clutched at her ass, feeling her strong inner muscles tighten repeatedly, as she came again and again. Feeling his control rapidly leaving him, his movements became shallow and quicker as he sought his release in her clenching heat. He strained for control yet realized he had lost. With a final surge of power, he ploughed into her with all of his strength, grunting triumphantly at her. "You're mine! Woman, you're mine!" He changed to a non-verbal roar as he shook with the repeated spasms of his bliss.

With his release, his legs threatened to collapse, and he leaned heavily against her, holding himself up by holding onto her. Quivering mass of jelly that he had made her become, she still managed to hold him up as they shook and trembled. Their tight embrace was all that allowed them to remember that they had bodies. Panting heavily, they both fought to control their shaking. They looked at each other for a long moment before they both laughed with the sheer joy of being together again.

"Can we do round two in a bed? I'm getting too old for this shit!" Marcus rasped out, trying to sound coherent.

Tenderly, she wiped the sweat off of his face before licking it off of her fingers. "I guess we could, old man. But don't think you're getting off easy due to your being older than me. Four years is not enough for me to cut you any slack. I expect you to pleasure me all night for allowing you to stay the night with me."

"One night?" he growled at her. "After what I spent on that

dinner? I don't think so." He smiled as he leaned forward to claim her lips again. Their tongues dueled briefly before he pulled back to continue. "I demand all three nights. It's a long weekend. You and I both need *this* more than we need to do anything else. Fuck your schoolwork—fuck the rest of the world. I need to spend time with you—I need you!"

She gave a long, exaggerated sigh. "You've always been such a demanding asshole. Okay. I guess I can take the whole weekend off—as long as you promise to make me scream all day and all night!"

He grinned at her. "Let's go fill your tub. It's barely adequate, but it'll do."

"You were only in the guest bathroom. There's a bigger one in the master bathroom."

"Let's go see, then, shall we?"

And they did.

CHAPTER EIGHT: A RECOMMITMENT

They went out for breakfast on Saturday morning, then returned to her apartment to make love again. After that they went out to the grocery store, since Marcus said he wanted to make her pancakes on Sunday morning and she didn't have what he needed in her kitchen. They bought some food, trying hard not to look like they had been having sex for the last few hours, yet failing completely.

"Everyone will know," she whispered to him as they walked through the freezer aisle. She was staring at his nipples, as he stared at hers, both of them affected less by the cold than by their nearness to each other.

They barely got the groceries back into her apartment before they ripped each other's clothes off and made love on the living room furniture. He had her bend over the arm of the couch, then he was sliding in and out of her, squeezing her nipples, biting her neck, and telling her how much he loved only her. Responding, she screamed his name and came repeatedly, from the sheer pleasure of feeling him inside of her again, his balls slapping on her ass.

Later, after they finally got the food put away, they decided that after spending the entire day making love, they were too exhausted to cook dinner. She ordered a pizza to be delivered and they watched old monster movies on TV while they ate, laughing at all of the scary parts. Just before she fell asleep, totally sated, spooned in his arms, he made a hissing, growling noise and pretended to bite her neck, since they'd been watching vampire movies. She shrieked and laughed, twisting to get out of his arms, but he was entirely too strong for her to fight for long. They both fell into the deep and dreamless sleep of the totally satisfied.

Sunday's breakfast found her amazed at his culinary skills.

"Where did you learn to make such good pancakes?" She was busy sliding another one to her plate.

He grinned at her, flourishing the spatula. "I have many skills that you will learn to appreciate."

"I'll bet you do." She tried to leer with her mouth stuffed with pancakes but was comically unsuccessful.

Not wanting to be outdone, she promised to make him a dinner that he would not forget.

Leering at her, he asked if she was on the menu.

She retorted that she was the low-fat dessert — and he was an insatiable sex-fiend.

Laughing, he caught her in his arms and reminded her that he was *her* insatiable sex-fiend, and that it was all her fault, since she made him that way.

Sunday night's dinner was a surprise for him. Despite her earlier somewhat unsuccessful culinary attempts in their college days, she had become a decent cook. The long cooking time required for stew allowed for much down-time, during which they repeatedly went down on each other. By the time they were done eating and cleaning up, they were both exhausted enough to fall into bed to sleep.

Marcus woke up hours later, not sure what had disturbed his sleep. Reaching out for Melanie, he realized she was not there, so he went looking for her. Feeling a chill in the air, he pulled the light blanket off of the bed. He wrapped himself up in it and went in search of his woman.

He found her standing in the picture window in the living room, looking up at the sky. His breath caught in his throat, as he took in the sight of the beautiful goddess who was standing totally nude, looking up at the moon.

She heard him, so was not surprised when he moved behind her, and wrapped her up in the blanket — and his arms. "Not able to sleep, my love?"

"No."

"Me neither, once I realized that you weren't there for me to hold onto anymore." He inhaled deeply, enjoying the scent of her wafting up from her hair.

"Marcus, what are we going to do now?" She pulled his arms closer around her.

"I know what I'd like to do now." He pushed his erection against her back, grinding himself against her.

"That's not what I mean." She turned her head up to look back at him over her shoulder. "I mean about us. What are we going to do now?"

Unwilling to let reality intrude upon their time, but recognizing her insistence, he sighed. "As soon as I get back to Chicago, I'm calling my lawyer again and telling him to give her whatever the hell she wants so that I can be a free man again. Free to marry the woman I was meant to be with — the only woman I have ever really loved."

"And then what? You can't have a marriage when you live six hours apart. Reason dictates that the one who makes less money should be the one who gives up their job and joins the bigger breadwinner."

He leaned his head forward and bit at her earlobe, whispering into her ear, "Maybe I'll get lucky and knock you up on the honeymoon. Then you can stay home and teach our children for a while."

"Where? In the city?" She spat out her words, distaste evident even in the dark.

He sighed. "It's not *all* like where I grew up, you know. Even Mama doesn't live there anymore. I bought her a nice big home, in a really nice neighborhood. I used to live in a penthouse. Now I'm in a condo near the hospital. But we can look until we find something that you like, then move there."

Her shudder was palpable. "Not in the city. Not with all of those people around me all the time. I can't live there."

"Okay. Then we'll find a place in the suburbs, where you can feel more at home."

"Then you'll have a long commute every day, and I'll be worried about you doing all of that driving. And you'll have trouble when you are on call, because you'll be so far away."

He turned her to face him, looking into her eye, with the moonlight making her glow like some dark-haired angel. "What do you want from me? What will make you happy? I'll give it to you, if it's at all possible. Just tell me what you want."

Her face crumpled, and her tears fell.

He held her close, not knowing what else to do.

"I don't know what I want. I want you, but I like it here. I want to be your wife. I want to have your babies. I want so much, but I don't know how we can make this work."

He held her for a long time, waiting for her tears to subside. "Afraid again, are you? It's intense—these feelings of ours. Even more so than when we were young."

"Yes." She was ashamed, yet grateful that he understood her.

"We'll work it out this time," he said firmly. "We have to."

"How?"

"I don't know, but we will. I won't lose you again, Melanie. It damn near killed me the last time. I can't live through that again. I won't. You're meant to be with me, and me with you. That's an undeniable fact. So we'll figure it out."

She sniffled into his chest as he held her close in the moonlight. "Promise me that you'll find us a way?"

His chest almost burst with the love he felt for this woman, as he answered her. "Yes. I will find a way to make *us* work."

Holding her so closely, he stopped ignoring the demands that his body was making on him for his attention. Pressing her against him with his hands on her backside, he made her aware of what he wanted.

Predictably, she responded to him. Reaching her arms down and around his ass; she dug her fingers into him before she turned her face upwards and licked his chest yet again, rubbing her face against him, aware of his every need, as she always was.

He reached a hand down to hold her face and tilt it up to his. "Look at me in the moonlight, my love. Let me see your face. Let me see how you feel about me, reflected in your eyes. Then let me see how you look when I make love to you— when I make you mine again."

His mouth claimed hers as they both sank to their knees in the moonlight, arms wrapped around each other, each one determined to make the other one know how essential they were for life, for happiness. And by the light of the moon, as they made smooth, passionate love, Marcus promised both Melanie and himself that he would find a way to make their relationship work. And she believed him. They both did.

Breakfast the next morning was a bittersweet affair. They still got to chat, to touch each other, to exchange longing glances, but they both knew Marcus had to leave soon. Traffic would be fierce on the last day of a three-day weekend and would get worse the closer he got to Chicago. They made love one last time right after breakfast, with the morning sun streaming in, giving promise of a bright future.

Marcus had brought in his suitcase for clothes, so he had to pack it back up. While he was in the living room doing that, he suddenly stopped and pulled a business card holder out of his suitcase and called Melanie over, from checking the bedroom one last time for errant clothing.

"Here, honey, take this." He handed her a card that he had been writing on.

"Your card? Handy if I have a heart attack, right? Did you put something in the pancakes that I don't know about?"

"Ha ha," he snorted at her. "I put my personal cell phone number on the back of it, so you can reach me anytime, anywhere."

"No more *Paging Dr. Jones*? Does the nurse just pull it out of your back pocket and hold it up to your ear so you can chat, while you're up to your elbows in someone's chest? Ew!"

"No. Don't be silly. I meant you can always reach me unless the phone is off. The only time I turn it off is when I'm in surgery. So there."

She smirked at him. "Or when you're with me, apparently. I haven't heard it ring in all of the time you've been here."

He looked up from packing and smiled, nodding at her. Once finished, he got up and looked around again.

She sighed before putting the card into her pocket and wrapping her arms around him, pulling him close. "I'm going to miss more than the wicked good sex with you, you know." She spoke into his chest. "I'm going to miss joking with you, talking with you, and seeing you naked."

He rubbed her back, trying not to make it turn sexual, but failing completely. "I'll text you, e-mail you, and call you. About the only thing I can't send you is my body, though if you'd like a nude picture, that can be arranged." He smiled wickedly.

"No." She sighed. "Just my luck someone would hack my mail and open it. Then I'd never get your picture back, and you'd find yourself being sent around the world with some lame tag-line, like *Hot and horny married men and the women (and men) who want them.*"

He grinned. "Maybe the resulting public humiliation would finally get me my divorce."

"Just go, Marcus. Go while I can still summon the strength to let you walk out my door, okay? Then I'll dig into my enormous pile of paperwork and try to stop thinking about our wonderful weekend."

With a final long kiss and lots of lingering glances, suffused with sadness, Marcus pulled out of the driveway and headed back to Chicago.

Melanie found herself writing the first poetry she had written since she got out of college. Putting her feelings into words and then putting them into the drawer of her nightstand helped her to put them aside so she could return to being Ms. McKee, long-suffering, hard-working teacher. She resolved to work on the poems again soon, and to share them with Marcus the next time she saw him.

CHAPTER NINE: FATE INTERVENES

Marcus rubbed his throbbing temples and tried not to yell into his phone at his long-suffering lawyer. "What do you mean she still won't sign? She's the one who filed in the first place! I've let her claim anything she wants. What the fuck else does she want from me?"

"Well, Marcus." The lawyer cleared his throat.

Marcus realized that was never a good sign, since it means the lawyer is going to tell you something you don't want to hear.

"She has changed her demands yet again. Now she says she won't sign unless we put a codicil in the divorce decree saying that she gets one half of your income as alimony."

"What?" Marcus failed at controlling his temper. "We were only married for a year! We've been in the process of getting a divorce for months. What the hell has she done to earn alimony?"

"It doesn't really matter how long you were married, I'm afraid. What matters in the eyes of the court is that you make a whole lot more money than she does, and thus you need to ensure that she continues to live in the style she became accustomed to during your marriage."

There was a long silence while Marcus contemplated just how long he might get in jail for strangling the woman. "Is there any rule about me calling her? Maybe I can talk some sense into her."

"Good luck with that one." His lawyer chortled. "Where you are concerned, she doesn't seem to have any sense. Oh, and Marcus, is there something you're not telling me, that I really should be aware of?"

Marcus was instantly on guard. "Like what?"

"She started making insinuations about another woman being involved, hinting that her recent obstinacy is due to her feeling that you've been cheating on her." The lawyer cleared his throat again. "That's really something I need to be aware of, if it's true."

Marcus sighed before deciding to come clean with the man who was taking the heat, so he wouldn't have to face his angry, soon-to-be-ex, in person. "Yes, there is someone. But I haven't seen her for months. I've been too busy with surgeries and appointments, and God-only-knows-what else. She lives way the hell up in northern Wisconsin—about a six-hour drive away."

"I see. And were you seeing her while you were married— I mean, before the separation began?"

"No. Before a couple of months ago, I hadn't seen her since college. That was ten years ago."

"Okay. Then whatever she thinks she can use can be answered by us, since it happened after the separation. Good."

"Is that all? Because I really think I'm going to call her and see if I can get her to be reasonable."

His lawyer snorted with laughter. "Good luck with that. And good night."

Marcus listened to the decisive beep as his lawyer hung up. He sat with his head in his hands for a while after that, feeling the ache of loneliness that threatened to drown him whenever he thought about how far away Melanie was. He really needed to get up there to see her again. He knew she would let him in the door this time. He just had to clear some time off of his schedule to make it happen.

He still didn't have any idea how to solve their other long-term problem of where they could live together, with both of them happy in the choice. *Maybe I can find a job in a city smaller than Chicago, but in Wisconsin? Maybe I can change careers and become a dairy farmer? Maybe pigs will grow wings and learn to fly?* He sighed again.

About the only thing he *had* managed to do was find an ex-patient who was a pilot of a small plane. The pilot usually flew up to Wisconsin — Madison in particular, in order to pick up and deliver organs for transplants. Since Marcus had assisted on some transplants, they spoke often enough for him to ask about the possibility of being flown up to the Minocqua area, to avoid the six hours of driving time. George was happy to do it, as long as Marcus didn't mind the cramped seating in his cargo plane. Now all he had to do was find the time to get up there.

Melanie, I really need to see you again, woman. Suddenly he had a feeling of foreboding. *What if I could never see her again? What if she doesn't want me anymore? What if — ?*

He dialed Shandra's number, in order to deal with the most pressing problem first.

"Hello," she answered. "Whoever you are, this better be damn important! It's really late and I was just going to bed."

"Oh really?" His voice had a silky tone. "Alone, I expect?"

"Marcus, what the hell do you want?"

"I want to talk to you, that's all." He gritted his teeth, trying to sound more polite than he felt.

"Talk to my lawyer."

"Wait, what's this shit about needing alimony? We were only married for a year. And in that year, you spent money like there was no tomorrow. Don't you have enough money of your own?"

"That's not the point."

"Then what is the point?" He counted to ten, still trying to hold onto his temper.

"The point is my lawyer is better than your lawyer. And I'm the woman who's being wronged, so I'm going to take your ass for everything I can get and then some!"

He finally lost the battle with his temper. "When did you become such a vindictive bitch?"

She yelled into his ear. "Don't *you* call *me* any names, you cheating pig!"

After ignoring the first few buzzes from his phone telling him that he had another call trying to come in, and needing to take a moment to cool down, Marcus coldly told her, "I have another call coming in. It might be an emergency. I'll have to put you on hold for a second."

Taking great pleasure in the squeal of anger that she made, he clicked the button to answer the other call. "Yes?"

"Is this Dr. Marcus Jones?"

"Yes."

"Oh good. Then this is the right number to reach you at. This is Nurse Slovak at Twin Lakes Community Hospital. I need to ask you about a patient of yours."

"How the hell did you get this number?" He yelled because he was still in the midst of an emotional upheaval. With great effort, he forced himself to modulate his voice in speaking with another medical professional. "If you need to talk to me about a patient, then call my answering service. That's what they are there for."

"I'm really sorry to call so late, Dr. Jones, but we think we may have a patient of yours who has been in a car accident. We're prepping her for surgery now. But while looking in her purse for her insurance card, we found your card with this number written on the back."

Marcus felt his blood run so cold he thought his heart had stopped pumping. Abject fear gripped at his guts as he listened to the nurse talk.

"If she is a patient of yours, then we will have to postpone surgery, because the only cardiac surgeon on call up here lives in Green Bay, and it will take him some time to get here."

"Who," Marcus croaked, then licked his lips and tried again. "Who is the patient?"

"A local high school English teacher, a Ms. Melanie McKee. Is she a patient of yours?"

"No," he said out loud, while his mind tried to deny what he was hearing. *She's the mother of my future children. She's my only reason for living. She's my life!* He wanted to scream, but he restrained himself with great effort. "Let me talk to the doctor in charge," he croaked, trying to make his voice sound normal.

"I'm sorry?" She was all professionalism. "He's prepping for surgery. He doesn't have time to come to the phone."

"I said, let me talk to the doctor in charge." His words sounded clipped and strained. "Now!"

"I see. One moment, Dr. Jones." She answered him icily. "I'll see if I can get him on the line."

Time passed — probably only a couple of minutes. But to Marcus, it felt like hours before he heard another voice on his phone.

"Dr. Stevenson here," said a calm, commanding voice.

"Yes, Dr. Stevenson. "This is Dr. Jones."

"I'm honored to speak with you, Dr. Jones. I was at the conference in Madison earlier this year. I saw you speak. How can I help you?"

"Maybe you can answer some questions for me." Marcus licked his lips, trying to force enough moisture to them to speak intelligibly, when all he wanted to do was pound something and scream. He was afraid of the answer yet needed to know. "How bad are Melanie's injuries?"

"Well, Dr. Jones, my nurse informs me that you told her Ms. McKee is not a patient of yours." The doctor cleared his throat, obviously uncomfortable with what he was going to say. "So the extent of her injuries is not really something I should be discussing with you. HIPPA and all — you understand."

"No, you don't understand. I need to know how badly she was hurt." His throat felt raw with unshed tears that threatened to take over his voice.

"Exactly what is your relationship to my patient, Dr. Jones?"

This was it—the moment that Melanie had been afraid of. But Marcus didn't hesitate for a moment, because he had to know. "We are—" his voice cracked. "We are old friends. From college. We're very close. That's why she has my private cell phone number."

There was a long silence at the other end of the phone, before the other man spoke. "I've seen you speak. I admire your work. But you never heard this from me."

"Agreed."

"She was in a small rental car and a drunk driver ran across the median, hitting her head on. She has some cracked ribs, lots of contusions, and probably a shattered femur. I think the airbag prevented a lot of injuries. We don't suspect a concussion, but we need to run some tests—for that, and to be sure that everything is all right in her chest and abdomen. There may be internal bleeding, so we have to get her into surgery pretty quickly. I'm really glad that there are no heart complications, because I don't want to wait long enough for our cardiologist to get here."

Marcus was quiet for a few minutes, trying to get his nerves under control.

"Dr. Jones?"

With great effort, he spoke again. "If you're still in surgery when I get there, may I observe?"

"You are in Chicago, aren't you? I certainly don't expect to be in surgery with her for six hours."

"I don't plan to drive. I'm going to fly. Can I observe?"

"Yes, of course. Not assist, since you have a personal

connection. But you are welcome in my surgical theater any-time you want to be here." Dr. Stevenson sounded warm and friendly, and apologetic. "I'm afraid I have to go now, since I am getting the signal that they're ready for me now."

"One more thing, please?" Marcus hated how needy his voice sounded.

"Yes?"

"What was the name of the hospital again?"

"Twin Lakes Community Hospital. It's the only one in Minocqua."

"Thank you very much, Dr. Stevenson. I'll be seeing you very soon."

"I look forward to meeting you." Dr. Stevenson hung up the phone.

Marcus sat and looked at his phone for a moment, then re-alized that the light was still blinking. *Of course. Shandra's still on the other line.* Reluctantly, he hit the button to return to her.

"It's about fucking time! Who do you think you are, mak-ing me wait so long?"

"I'm sorry, Shandra, but there's been an emergency. I have to go now."

"What? You called me, you asshole! And made me wait. I won't stand for this bullshit—"

He hung up on her. Then he called his friend with the plane.

The plane ride up was a blur. Once George understood Marcus needed a ride up north immediately, he made the ar-rangements and met him at the Pal-waukee airport. Marcus didn't have any compunction about telling those he needed to help him about how important Melanie was to him. He didn't have to. It was in his voice, his face, his every move-ment. He packed faster than he would have thought was pos-sible and called his secretary from the car. He told her he had a family emergency. He asked her to cancel all of his appointments for the next three days and not to refer any calls to him for the same time period.

All told, it took him an hour to get into the air, then a little over an hour to fly up across six hours of country roads. During all of that time, Marcus was doing something he rarely did—something he hadn't relied on since he became a man. He prayed. *Please God, keep her safe. Don't take her away from me. I need her. I love her. I can't live without her. Please.* The words played themselves over and over in his mind until it became a mantra.

Once in the local Minocqua airport, Marcus quickly commandeered a rental car, acutely aware of the irony that his woman had been injured in one, but he needed one to get to her side. He got directions to the hospital from the rental agent and drove way too fast to get there.

When he finally got to the hospital, he had to deal with the nurse in charge. She balked at letting him up to where he wanted to go. Finally he remembered the name of the nurse who had called him originally and was grimly pleased to note that her name brought immediate action from everyone. He also tossed in the name of Dr. Stevenson, who he learned was the head of the hospital and of the surgical department, and who had been on call that night. Once they gave him an ID and the proper directions, he soon found himself standing outside of the operating room where Melanie was.

Looking into the window he saw that the surgeon was finishing up, but he went to the scrub room anyway, in order to be able to see her as soon as possible. He met Dr. Stevenson doing his post-operation scrubbing. The other man recognized him and told him what he wanted to hear. "She has three broken ribs—one had punctured her left lung. Good thing there weren't any cardiac complications. No other internal bleeding. Shattered femur, as I thought. Hairline fracture in her left arm. No signs of concussion that we could find. I think she'll be fine, once she does a whole lot of healing."

Marcus grabbed the end of the sink, holding himself up, weak with relief. "Can I go see her?"

"Of course! You're welcome to go anywhere in my hospital that you want to go," Dr. Stevenson told him warmly. "In fact, once you're done making sure that we did a good-enough job patching her up, why don't you ask for directions to my office?"

"Yes. I'll do that."

Marcus steadied his nerves and went to check on Melanie. The recovery room was like any other one he had ever been in. The only difference was how much he cared about the recovery of *this* patient. Intensely unhappy because he couldn't touch anything, he watched as Melanie breathed with great difficulty and pain. Her face, drawn and white, made him fear the worst, even though her doctor's reassuring words echoed in his head. The small moans she made cut him to the quick. Even though he knew he was not supposed to touch her, he leaned over and kissed her lips, whispering to her, "I'm here, honey. I'm not leaving. I love you."

When the nurse shook her head at him firmly, clearly not used to civilians in her recovery ward, he turned and left the room. Asking a few people, he found the way to Dr. Stevenson's office relatively easily. It might be a big hospital by northern Wisconsin standards, but it was nowhere near as huge and complicated to maneuver around in as what he was used to.

He found Dr. Stevenson sitting at his desk perusing paperwork. The older man looked up when he entered and rose with a smile to warmly shake his hand. "Dr. Jones? To formally introduce myself, I'm Dr. Stevenson. Call me Joe."

"Just call me Marcus. I'm greatly in your debt for allowing me to see her so soon after surgery. I can't tell you how much that means to my piece of mind."

"You *do* look a bit ragged around the edges," the older man observed. "Are you a scotch drinker, Marcus?"

"On occasion. But right about now, I would drink rubbing alcohol, if it was offered."

Joe Stevenson smiled at him, taking a key out of his pocket, and opening one of the drawers. He looked up and winked as he pulled a bottle that was hidden behind some files out of his bottom drawer. "I keep the good stuff down here, so my meddlesome secretary doesn't know where it is. There are times, Marcus, as I'm sure you know, that a shot of scotch is the best medicine for a surgeon." He poured a shot into each of two glasses he took out of the same drawer. He gave one to Marcus and toasted him with it. "To professional courtesy. May it help us all when we need it."

"Amen." Marcus sipped the potent brew, then smiled and nodded at his host, who was watching to see if he approved. "So are you the director of this hospital, as well as the chief surgeon?"

"Yes."

"And still you get stuck doing emergency surgeries this late at night?"

Joe smiled at him. "We aren't a big city operation like you're used to. The lines between administration and practicing medicine are not as stringent up here."

"What's your special area?" Marcus asked, curious about the man who'd had his hands in Melanie's precious body.

"General internal medicine. I trained as a general surgeon. I got another degree in administration, because there was a need once the last chief of surgery retired."

"So you wear two hats around here?"

Joe laughed. "I wear as many hats as they need me to wear around here."

"But you don't have a cardiologist?"

"No. We share him with Green Bay."

"Why?"

"Because we can't afford one of our own. You specialty guys cost too damn much money."

"Oh," was all that Marcus' tired brain could reply. An idea was trying to present itself to him, but he was just too damn exhausted to hear it. "Is there anywhere I can sleep in the hospital, until she gets out of recovery?"

"Yes, in the doctors' room, of course. I take it you are familiar with them?" There was a twinkle in the older man's eye, both a challenge and an acknowledgement that they had both spent more time than they ever wanted to in doctors' sleeping rooms. "However, there is a motel right up the road a piece."

"No." Marcus shook his head. "I know what you people mean by *up the road a piece*. I'd rather stay right here, so I can be here when she wakes up."

Joe shrugged. "Suit yourself. That won't be for quite a few hours, you know. But I'll tell Nurse Slovak to make sure to wake you when she does."

Marcus groaned. "I presume she'll accept my apology for being so rude on the phone?"

Joe grinned. "She likes milk chocolates, no nuts."

Marcus let Joe lead the way to the doctors' sleeping room. He was pleased to find that his overnight bag was already there. Since he had dropped it at the scrubbing room door, he looked at Joe curiously.

"I told you she's very efficient. And observant. She might not ever have had chocolates from Chicago, so Fannie May might make her very happy." Joe left to go back to doing his job.

Marcus found a bed to lie down in. He spent some time tossing and turning. Finally willing his body to rest, he slept fitfully for a few hours.

CHAPTER TEN: GRIST FOR THE GOSSIP MILL

Melanie fought her way up out of what seemed to be a long tunnel, dark on all sides, but relatively pain-free. Once her mind registered consciousness, she became aware of intense pain. It hurt to breathe, it hurt to not breathe. Her body ached all over, and she was aware of the sensation of IVs in her arms. *Yuck! Is that a catheter stuck all up in there, as well?*

She tried to remember how she had been brought to this pain. She remembered that her truck had been shaking for weeks, and that she had finally taken it in, only to find it was a major problem that needed immediate attention. Since she needed to get around, at least to work and back, she had reluctantly taken the only loaner on the lot, a small sedan. It was as low as Marcus' Jaguar, but not nearly as much fun to drive. It didn't want to respond to her foot on the gas pedal, nor did it really want to brake when she wanted it to. Never-the-less, it was a vehicle. And the service department promised to have her truck done in a couple of days.

She frowned, remembering leaving school really late after a particularly long evening spent with the students, working on the literary magazine. She had been hungry, tired, and anxious to get home, hoping to find an e-mail, or phone call from Marcus. After all of these years, she still got a special tingle out of Tuesday nights—as if that mattered anymore.

There was a car heading too fast in the other direction. It started jumping across the median and heading right for me. Yikes! No wonder I'm in so much pain. I'm lucky to be alive.

Slowly she tried moving her arms—first one, then the other. When they both responded, though with pain on one side, she tried her legs as well. One appeared to be in a cast, but she was able to wriggle her toes, so she was relatively reassured that she was probably not paralyzed.

With great effort, she opened her eyes. Her head was facing towards her left, where she could see, beyond a half-drawn curtain, the light coming from the hall. The door was almost closed, so the noise from beyond was muted. She considered trying to call out to someone but found that it was difficult to swallow, since her throat was so dry. She hadn't been in a hospital as a patient since she'd had her tonsils out when she was five years old, but she remembered being really thirsty then also. She wondered if that was all a part of the patient experience. *Why doesn't someone sell some kind of breath freshener to spray into the mouths of unconscious patients, so at least we wake up feeling refreshed from tingly, halitosis-free breath?*

She tried to chuckle, but all she could do was croak. She decided to turn her head and look in the other direction. *Yes! My head turns okay, so my neck can't be broken. I can feel my feet, so my back's probably okay. But everything hurts.*

She became aware that her right hand was being held by someone. Turning her head all the way to the right, she was shocked to see Marcus sitting in a chair next to her bed. His head was lolled back as he snored softly.

Oh my God! Why is he here? My heart? Is there something wrong with my heart? She felt that heart start to pound with fear. Sweat prickled at her neck. "Marcus," she croaked painfully.

Instantly his head jerked forward and his eyes opened. His fingers curled more tightly around hers and he smiled. "Sleeping Beauty awakens." He leaned forward to search her face. "How are you feeling, my love?"

"Like I got hit by a fucking truck."

"Actually I was told it was smaller than a truck, but bigger than that puny rental car they stuck you in." He glowered menacingly. "I hope the guy who put you into that thing has a heart attack someday, so I can refuse to save his unworthy ass."

She attempted a smile but found her lips too dry to move around much.

Marcus picked up a small glass of water from the table next to her bed and held the straw to her lips, telling her, "Only a small sip. Doctor's orders."

Gratefully, she sipped. She watched him put the glass back down. Her brow furrowed. "Did I have a heart attack after it?"

His eyebrows rose in surprise as he shook his head. "No. Your heart was not involved. Mine was, though."

"I knew I wasn't in heaven because everything hurts too much. I knew I wasn't in hell because you're here. But *why* are you here?"

"Because I was smart enough to give you a business card with my personal cell number on the back, and you were smart enough to carry it around with you, that's why."

She looked confused.

"They called me after you were brought in. They found my card and thought that you were a patient of mine. They called to see if they needed to delay surgery to wait for a cardiologist to assist. I flew straight up but didn't get here until after you were out of surgery."

"So you didn't get to look inside of me, then?" She was trying to tease, but failed, since her voice was just a dry croak.

He touched her face tenderly. "I already love you inside and out. I don't need to know anything else about you. But I needed to be here, to be sure that you were being taken good care of. And you are."

"Good," she said wearily, as the drugs in her IV bag and

the tiredness in her body united to make her unable to remain awake. "I love you, Marcus. Now go home before someone realizes who you are and I get to be the centerfold in *Mistresses of the Month* magazine."

He snorted softly, still stroking her face and her hair. "Not a chance, honey. I'm here until I feel like leaving." He watched her for a long time as she drifted back to sleep. Then he went out to the hall to inform the nurses that she had awoken briefly. Letting them go in to do their job, he went in search of Joe Stevenson, to get the promised tour of the hospital. The idea that had been trying to bring itself to his conscious mind was beginning to percolate. He needed to see for himself if it presented a possibility of fruition.

After the tour, Marcus was not surprised when Joe asked him to accompany him to dinner. He asked what Mrs. Stevenson would think about that, but Joe pointed out that the Mrs. was in Florida, visiting her mother, so he had to find his own dinner. After discovering that they both liked Thai food, Marcus was amazed to be taken to a hole-in-the-wall place that had excellent Pad Thai. They both had to gulp their beers to cool the burn,

"My admiration for your town grows." Marcus was busy wiping the sweat off his face, from their authentic-style dinners.

Joe invited Marcus to continue their evening in a local bar. As they walked in, Marcus saw bottles of single malt scotch lining the mirror behind the bar, along with a deer head, and crossed rifles.

"Are Black men allowed in here?" Marcus was only half-joking.

Joe shook his head, grinning. "Of course. Look around you."

Marcus did, and found that his was not the only dark skin

in the place. There were other Black faces, some that looked Asian, some Hispanic — and some men who looked like Native Americans were shooting pool.

"We're not in the south, you know. We're really far north of the Mason-Dixon Line up here."

"Yeah, but I've never spent any time this far north. In fact, I've never spent much time out of Chicago, except when I was in college, down in DeKalb."

"I presume that's where you met Ms. McKee."

Marcus nodded.

Their scotches were delivered. They both spent a moment admiring the amber color in their glasses before they reverently took sips.

The older man studied Marcus for a moment before he took a deep breath. "Why don't we stop beating around the bush, and get to business?"

"Business?"

"Yes, business. You're a famous cardiologist. My hospital could really use your skills. I could never afford to pay you what you're worth. However, you appear to be in love with a local gal. That's a pretty valuable trump card I hold. So, what would it take to get you to say *Yes*?"

Marcus thought for a long moment. "Do you get many heart patients up here?"

"Oh Lord, yes! We're a pretty sizable town, even without tourists, for being this far north. But our population grows a lot, especially in the spring, summer, fall times of year. We're a mecca for outdoor recreational activities. Campers and hunters come up here year-round. And even in the winter, they come up here for ice fishing. They come from all over, but they always seem to have their heart attacks up here. We have to send the ones who are not urgent to Green Bay, since that's where our on-call guy lives. For the really critical ones, he travels here."

"Hmmm." Marcus looked at his glass again.

"But I would have to ask you to do other surgeries sometimes. We can't afford someone so specialized that they wouldn't take their turn doing the overnighters or the on-call surgeries that come up when you least expect them." Joe paused significantly. "Like from car accidents."

Marcus took another drink. "How many of you are there? To take your turns?"

"Well, I'm the head general surgeon, and there are two more surgeons besides me. Mary's our OB-gynecologist, Sherry is the pediatrician, Craig is the endocrine-specialist, and Luke is the bone-setter. We have all gotten good at covering each other's backs. We've been doing this for years, with the cardiologist on call from miles away. Between the seven of us, we take care of the place, twenty-four-seven. But I'm not lying to you when I say we could really use your skills around here."

Marcus studied his scotch while he swirled it around in the glass. "What kind of offer are we talking about?"

Joe wrote a number on a cocktail napkin and pushed it across the table.

Marcus raised an eyebrow, before putting it into his pocket. "Let me think about this for a while."

Joe nodded. "I might be able to increase it a little, if that's what it takes to get to a *yes*. I'd have to take that up with the hospital board first, though. You just take all of the time you need. We've gone this long without you. We'll do fine if you say *No*. But we'll do even better if you say *Yes*."

The conversation switched to more casual topics, like politics, the environment and the benefits of single-malt versus blended scotches. Since they both knew how to shoot pool, they spent some time in the next room, trying to impress each other with their skills.

Finally, after missing yet another shot, Marcus laughed. "If

Melanie was here, she'd wipe up the table with both of our sorry asses."

Joe shook his head, grinning. "She's good at pool also? Not surprising, I guess. She seems to be good at a lot of things. She taught both of my boys. I don't know who had the bigger crush on her—them or me. Whenever I had to go to the school on their behalf, it was all I could do to focus on what she was talking about instead of how good-looking their English teacher was."

Marcus nodded. "Yeah, she's one fine-looking woman. I'm in your debt for saving her life. Now you've given me something to think about. I think we should call it a night. I'll need a ride back to the hospital so I can sleep in her room again."

Joe dropped him off at the main entrance, then drove off.

Once back in the hospital, long-since used to the twenty-four-hour atmosphere of wakefulness, Marcus showed his badge before making his way back up to Melanie's room. She slept on, oblivious to what he was planning to ponder as he watched her sleep.

"I promise I'll be up to see you as soon as I can." Marcus was holding Melanie's hand again. He had come back to her room to say goodbye, since his three days was up and George had promised to get him back to Chicago for a scheduled surgery.

"The next time off I'll be getting is spring break. That's the last week of March." Melanie's voice sounded stronger after a couple of days spent recovering. "That's a little over a month from now."

"I'll see what I can do." Marcus made a mental note to fall off the edge of the planet if he had to so he could get a chance to be with her for a whole week.

"Do you think I'll be well enough to entertain you by then?" Melanie had a spark of her old self inherent in her raised eyebrows.

"Well, I'll have to do a very thorough examination, to be sure." Marcus leered back at her. "But I think, as an experienced doctor, I'll be able to be gentle when needed."

"Too bad we can't push the limits and get some real use out of my adjustable hospital bed."

Marcus peered intently into her face, then laughed at how serious she looked. "You must be joking! You are—aren't you?"

Melanie gave him an innocent smile. "Maybe. But then, if I could make a guy in a body cast smile without re-breaking his back, I don't see why you can't make us both smile before you leave."

Marcus snorted a short burst of laughter before studying her face. "You aren't joking. You're really serious." He sighed at the smug look on her face.

"I know I'm going to regret this, because I probably don't really want to know the details. But as a medical man, I want to know. And as the last man you are ever going to have sex with, I need to know. What's the story?"

"Well, it was way before I met you," she began with a smile.

Marcus raised his eyebrows at her. "They weren't all, but go on."

"He was a guy I picked up one night, and we had a brief fling over the next week or so. It was fun recreational sex. There were no real feelings on the part of either of us, so we parted as friends. We'd chat briefly when we'd see each other in the bars."

"Um-hmm."

"So when I saw him in the bar this one time, I went over to say *hello*. When I got close, I noticed he looked kind of weird. I sat on the barstool next to him and realized that he had a cast sticking up out of the top of his shirt. *Holy crap! What happened to you?* I asked him. He told me he had been in a car accident, and some of his vertebrae had been fractured. He had to wear the cast for a few months, but he was just glad he wasn't paralyzed. So I bought him a beer and we sat and chatted about nothing in particular for a while. Finally I leaned over and whispered in his ear, 'So, are you getting any these days?' He laughed. 'You're kidding, right? I'm in a fucking body cast! No, I'm not getting any — not for a long time.'

Marcus shook his head. "You're probably the only woman I know who would ask him that."

Melanie nodded. "That's what he said, too. Anyway, I licked his ear and told him that if he was game, so was I. He got up so fast he almost fell over. It didn't take us long to walk to my apartment. We got right to it. He was on the bottom — I was very careful not to push down too hard on him. But it was, shall we say, a real experience? I was kind of scared that I was gonna re-break his back, but I didn't. And let's just say the look of gratitude on his face afterward was really satisfying and made up for it only being an *okay* experience for me."

Marcus shook his head again, smiling.

"I saw him a year or so later, but by then he had discovered that he was gay. He still bought me a beer. The last I heard he was studying to become an ordained minister and had moved out to California." Melanie shrugged casually, grimacing when pain shot through her shoulder. "So as you can see, I have had experience with these things, Marcus. I'm not in a body cast, so how difficult would it be for us to sneak a little quickie in, while the nurses are busy elsewhere?"

Marcus snorted. "Honey, you're not the one with a medical reputation to uphold. I don't think it would look so good on my resume if *had sex with a patient in a hospital bed* was added."

"But I'm not *your* patient."

"No, but the other doctors here know who I am. I can't risk

it. Besides, I thought you were all for keeping our relationship a secret?"

Melanie shook her head. "I don't think it's much of a secret anymore. But fine, you go back to your life in Chicago, and I'll get on with the business of recovering."

"I don't have a life in Chicago—just an existence." Marcus observed. "The only time I feel really alive is when I'm with you."

"That's so sweet, Marcus." She sighed and held out her good arm, to encourage him to hug, as well as kiss her. "Then goodbye, sweetie."

Marcus sat on the bed and gently took her into his arms, careful not to hurt her. He used one hand to tilt her head upwards and kissed her. The kiss was gentle at first, then got more urgent. With a groan, he stood up quickly. "Enough! Even when you're injured, you still make my blood boil. I'm leaving for your own good. For the good of both of us." He strode quickly away from her. At the door, he turned back, to smile and wave, then he walked down the hall.

Melanie sighed. She closed her eyes to imagine what they would do to celebrate being together, once she was healed and he was back in town.

Chapter Eleven: A New Path to Pleasure

Once she got out of her week's stay at the hospital, Melanie was given three weeks off work to convalesce from her injuries. She took the time to catch up on all of her grading and to plan ahead a little bit, so that she would be able to take spring break off of work entirely.

The first week back at work was so tiring that she had to go to bed almost immediately every night when she got home. The second week was a bit better. And on Tuesday night she rushed to get the phone when it rang later than usual, long after dinner. She was done loading the day's dishes into the dishwasher, done with her shower, and starting on her grading.

"Hello." She panted into the phone.

"That breathlessness better be because you were running a marathon to get back into shape for my visit." Marcus was obviously only half-joking, since it was easy to be jealous with so many miles between them.

"Ha ha! Very funny." Melanie snorted into the phone. "I'll just tell the boys who were here for private lessons on enacting the balcony scene of *Romeo and Juliet* to wait in the next room while we chat, okay?"

Marcus moaned. "Youth and stamina—and they're right there with you. How can I hope to compete with that?"

"You're being silly." She scoffed into the phone. "You're the only man for me. In fact, everyone in town knows it now.

Why, it was on the front page of the local paper just last week."

"So does that mean that next time I don't have to rent a motel room that I don't intend to sleep in?"

"No." She sighed. "My reputation is already trashed. This is still very much a small town. Everyone in the hospital knew who you were there to visit, and they told everyone they know the next day. By the second day after I was injured, those in the know made sure that damn near everyone in town knew about the famous rich Chicago doctor who flew up here to check on lil' ol' me."

"Am I supposed to say I'm sorry now?" Marcus's tone was defiant. "Because I'm not, you know. I had to see for myself how you were and make sure that you were in good hands. Which you were. Otherwise, I'd have had you flown back down here to get the care you deserve."

"Ooh, baby, you say the nicest things! You get me so hot when you get all protective and stuff."

"Honey, are you sitting down?" Marcus abruptly changed the subject.

"Yeah, why?" Melanie sounded suspicious.

"Because I want to talk dirty to you for a while. I'm so horny I can't even see straight. Maybe I can make myself come, maybe not. But I know for a fact that I'm having trouble concentrating. I can't allow my job performance to be off even the slightest. Not while I'm trying to get my schedule cleared for your break—not to mention working on that other problem of ours, finding a place we can live together where we'll both be happy."

"Okay." Melanie sounded hesitant. "But I've never done it over the phone. I don't really know how."

"Actually, neither have I. But I really need you now, and we're too far away to do anything else."

"So how do we start?"

"What are you wearing?" Marcus tried to make his voice sound low and sexy.

Melanie giggled. "You sound like Barry White. Or the start to an obscene phone call in a bad horror movie."

"I was trying to sound sexy." Marcus sounded wounded. "I don't know how to do this either."

"Okay, okay. I'm not wearing anything special—just flannel pajama pants and an old tee shirt. All I was planning on doing was grading papers."

"Why don't you go sit on your bed and talk to me from there?" Marcus suggested.

"Just a minute." She followed his instructions. "All right. I'm on my bed now, sitting back against the headboard. Now what?"

"I'm sitting in my computer chair, and it's fully adjustable. I'd really love to have you on my lap right about now, so I could sink myself into your hot pussy."

"Ooh, I'm starting to get really hot now, too." Melanie purred into the phone. "So, what are *you* wearing?"

"Only a pair of boxer shorts."

"Silk?"

"Yes."

"Oh God . . ."

"Why don't you take off your shirt and touch those beautiful breasts of yours? Like I wish I was doing?" Marcus was breathing heavier into the phone.

"I am." Melanie was breathing faster also.

"Tell me what you're doing and how it feels."

"I'm stroking the nipples and twisting them, pretending that it's your mouth doing it."

"Yes, it would be, because I love to play with your tits. Now take off your pants too, so I can smell you over the phone."

"You really are a bad boy, aren't you?" Melanie asked in a

breathy tone.

"Yes I am. Are you a bad girl, too?"

"Yes I am. In fact, without you even telling me to, I'm touching myself *down there*, like you would if you were here."

"Now dip your finger into your pussy, then taste it—tell me what you are thinking." Marcus was having real trouble making clear words.

"Ooh! Baby! Feels so good."

"Now listen to me, Melanie." Marcus paused. "What you are smelling and tasting is why I call you *honey*. I don't want you remembering that asshole you used to date so long ago. In fact, I don't want you thinking about other men at all. I just want you to remember that to me, you taste like the finest honey I have ever had the privilege to have in my mouth."

He heard the sound of a long breath being sucked in, followed by a sigh. Marcus knew that she had come for the first time already. He increased the speed and pressure of his stroking, trying to maintain enough blood in his brain to keep talking. "Now put your finger even deeper into yourself, honey." His voice was ragged. "How does that feel?"

"Not nearly as good as when it's your finger, but it's making me even hotter."

"Do you feel how your muscles grip so strong? So tight that I have to fight myself not to come the instant I'm in your body?"

"Yes." She seemed distant, not really listening to him anymore. "I can feel myself gripping my fingers. I'm stroking in and out, in and out. Oh God, I'm going to come again!"

At the sound of her small shriek, Marcus pumped himself, lost control, and gave himself over to the orgasm that was intense enough to make him groan.

"Was it good for you, too?" She gasped into the phone.

"Yes." He was trying to get his breath back to normal.

"Well, then, Dr. Marcus. I think we finally found something to share that we were both virgins at."

He chuckled at her tone. "Honey, everything I do with you feels like the first time. And it also feels like I've been doing it with you forever. You are the best at everything. You know what I want even before I do. That's why I love you so much."

"Not for my erudite wit? My sterling sense of humor? My bewildering intelligence?"

"No," he spoke softly. "That stuff is all enjoyable — a part of the *package of you*. But I first fell for your sensuality, your uninhibited enjoyment of everywhere I touch you, and your honey."

"Marcus, you really know how to woo a woman." Melanie cleared her throat. "I hate to sound so crass, but I love you for your cock that fits into me so perfectly. Not too big, so I'm sore all the time — not too small, so I don't notice it. You're like that *Three Bears* fairy tale. You're just right."

He groaned. "Stop! I said I wanted to come, but not more than once. I need to get some sleep. I have a surgery scheduled for six a.m. Have mercy, woman."

She giggled. "So when can I expect you here for spring break? The Friday it officially starts, I hope?"

"Um, yeah," He took a deep breath. "But I won't be there until around seven at night. I have a late appointment that will keep me from getting to you any earlier."

"Well then, just plan on me taking care of dinner, like the old days, okay?"

"Just for that one night — okay. But since we have a whole week, I plan to wine and dine you every night before I bed you. Then I'll feed you some more, then make love to you over and over again. Just so you know what to expect."

"Until then, I'll work really hard on my recovery, so I'm up to my usual standards. Wouldn't want to disappoint you, since you're going through so much trouble to be up here."

"I don't think it's possible for you to disappoint me, darlin'. But I'm going to say *good night* now, and hope to catch a few hours' sleep. You should also. You need your rest in order to heal."

"Believe me, dude, what we just did over the phone has done more than anything any other doctor has prescribed to make me feel better!"

"Good night, my love. Dream of me." Marcus commanded.

"Always." Melanie's voice sounded dreamy and sleepy. "Your every wish is my command. Good night, lover."

They both hung up, and shortly afterward they both fell asleep—not sated but having had the worst of the pressure of being separated temporarily relieved.

Chapter Twelve: Homecoming

Three weeks later, Marcus drove as fast as he dared from the late afternoon appointment with Dr. Stevenson to make it to Melanie's place by seven pm. He had been somewhat distracted during their conference as they attempted to reach an agreement they could both be comfortable with. He was having real trouble, as he had for days, concentrating on anything other than how many hours, now minutes, before he would be with Melanie again. But he had wanted to have enough of the plans finalized so that he could share the good news with her.

Dr. Stevenson smiled. Once they had shaken hands to signal a final agreement had been made, he told Marcus, "Go, get the hell out of my office. Go thank my *trump card* for delivering you to my hospital."

Knowing how pissed she would be for having been referred to like that, Marcus made a mental note to *not* tell her that. Then he hit the road and flew to her place, praying he wouldn't get a ticket, since that would slow him down too much. It was only five minutes after seven pm when he knocked on her door, his overnight bag over one shoulder, his other hand holding a wrapped box full of some sexy lingerie that he hoped to talk her into at his first opportunity.

He was surprised when he heard the door being unlocked, but not opened. He heard, "Come into my parlor, Marcus." He realized she had seen him through the peep hole. He pushed the door open and walked into an empty room. Suddenly the door was slammed shut and locked, and he felt his shoulder bag being pulled off. He turned in time to see a blur of naked white flesh, before she pressed herself against him, forcing his head down. "At last!"

He dropped the gift box. They were kissing, tongues dueling, and he was touching her skin everywhere, remembering — fondling — groaning. She tore at his shirt, trying to get it off him while remaining plastered to his body. He let her go and pulled his shirt over his head in a smooth move that made her suck in her breath as his stomach muscles rippled.

Immediately she was on him again, licking, sucking, biting, rubbing her face on his chest, in the indent in-between his nipples, biting the hair that grew there, marking him again as hers. She fell to her knees in front of him and kissed and bit at his thighs, while she opened his zipper, then slowly pulled his pants down, taking care to blow her hot breath on, and nuzzle his straining erection. She pulled off his shoes and watched as he stepped out of his pants. Then she began to lick at him through the silk boxers he had worn for her. Her mouth teased him unmercifully, alternately blowing hot air on him, then taking him in her mouth through the silk, to lick and suck on him, until he felt his knees begin to buckle.

She pushed him backwards, crawling after him like some kind of sexy wild animal, growling, until he felt his ass connect with the sofa — the same one that he had bent her over to make her scream on his last visit. He sat down and she pulled his boxers down, taking him in her mouth until her nose was smashed against him. She forcefully gulped again and again, until the tightness of her throat as she worked him and the saliva that she was swirling around him with her tongue made him lose all semblance of control. He dug his fingers into her scalp and howled his orgasm, pumping himself into her. She choked, then recovered, continuing to lick and suck at him, long after he felt like he had lost consciousness.

Finally she lay her head down on his thigh, content to

nuzzle him, smell him, and occasionally nip and bite him.

Just as he mind began to clear and he approached being able to speak, she licked and sucked him back into engorgement, smiling as he moaned. "Welcome home, Marcus!" She wrapped her arms around him, massaging his buttocks with her fingers, working them up his back. She tore open a package with her teeth, then slid a nubby condom onto him,

He put his hands on her shoulders and drew her up to sit on his lap, straddling his thighs. "Oh Lord! Woman, you're trying to kill me."

He ran his hands all over her, paying special attention to the hard nipples on her flushed breasts, and finally dipping down into her curls to find she was ready for him, as she always was. He began to suck on her hard pink nipples, first one then the other. She moaned. He slid himself into her waiting heat, hardening more with every stroke until he felt her quiver, then she threw her head back and screamed her pleasure at the return of her man.

Sometime later, when they were finally sated enough to notice being hungry, Melanie ordered a pizza. They opened some cold beers and sat on the couch discussing their plans for the week while they waited for the food to arrive. Marcus insisted on paying, but Melanie had to slip on some clothes to answer the door — and not the ones in the gift box that Marcus had just let her open.

Marcus waited until they were done satisfying their food hunger before he told her he had something to tell her.

Melanie leaned back against the couch and watched as he mentally prepared himself to share his news.

"My divorce should be finalized by the time the school year ends."

"Good."

"But that's not the real news."

"No?"

"I have a confession to make. The appointment that I had today was here in town, with Dr. Stevenson at Twin Lakes."

"Why?"

"You're looking at the future head of the newly-created Cardiology department at Twin Lakes."

"You're joking, right?"

"No, I'm serious. We had done most of the negotiating over the phone and e-mail, but today we finalized the details and I signed the contract. I'm giving ten weeks' notice. I'll be out of the University of Chicago by the middle of June."

"You're giving up your career for me? I'm not sure that's such a good idea."

He laughed, leaning forward to grasp both of her hands in his. "What the hell? You're the one who won't move down to Chicago with me. And besides, I'm not giving up my career. I'm just adapting it—changing back to what I originally thought a career in medicine would be all about."

"But you hate being in the middle of butt-fuck nowhere!"

"Honey, the only thing I hate more is having to live without you. Besides, as I told you, I've been bored lately, working on the elderly idle rich, making sure they can make it to their next golf outing or charity ball. Up here I'll have a chance to use more of my talents, to benefit more people."

She sat back, leaning away from him, talking in a quiet voice. "Won't you come to resent me for making you give up what you have down there for a life up here in the middle of butt-fuck nowhere?"

"As long as life up here has you in it, I can deal with anything. I told you, there's no life for me down there if you are up here. My life is where you are. You won't move to Chicago—so the only other option is I move up here."

"You won't make as much money, will you?"

"No. But I paid off my student loans a long time ago. Plus

the cost of living is lower up here. Besides, until I start keeping you barefoot and pregnant all the time, we can bank what you make."

She was silent for such a long time that he began to worry that she had somehow changed her mind and didn't want to start a new life with him in it. Finally unable to wait any longer for her to talk first, he took both of her hands in his and hesitantly asked her, "Is there something wrong? Don't you like my surprise?"

She raised her head to look at him, and the tears in her eyes, combined with the softness of her expression, suffused her face with love and adoration. "Like it? I'm shocked speechless! And you, of all people, know how hard that is to do. I'm humbled by the extent of your love, and inordinately grateful that it is *me* that you love so much. I want you in my bed every night for the rest of our lives, and the knowledge that you want me that much, even after all we've been through, makes me wonder how I can express my joy when I've already given you the blow-job of a lifetime."

Marcus let out the breath he hadn't realized he'd been holding. He leaned forward to kiss her, then let his lips trail along her neck to her earlobe. He whispered into her ear, "Just put on some of that lingerie I bought for you, and let me tear it off of you with my teeth. We'll call it even. Deal?"

"Then can we soak in my tub, to finalize the deal?"

"Done."

And in due time, it was.

CHAPTER THIRTEEN: MARCUS MAKES PLANS FOR THEIR FUTURE

In retrospect, Shandra realized she should have known something was up when she walked into the judge's chambers to see Marcus smiling like a Cheshire Cat. He and his lawyer had gotten there first, and they both rose to greet her and her lawyer. Handshakes all around.

"Let's be civilized about this, shall we?" he said before settling down at the round table with the judge.

Her first thought was that he was smiling because he had gotten laid recently. The private detective she had following him had reported that he had gone to Wisconsin for a week to see that slut he knew from college. The detective had made inquiries as to what kind of woman she was, after the first time he followed Marcus up there. After talking to just a few alumni who remembered her, he had reported that it was no good asking whom she had slept with—better to ask whom she had *not* had sex with, since that would be a much shorter list. Shandra was shocked. But since Marcus had not gone up to Wisconsin until after the divorce proceedings had begun, there really was no way to use his questionable taste in women against him.

Besides, Shandra herself had begun a relationship with one of the full partners who had recently been divorced, so she was now anxious to get the whole thing over with. The joy she'd been taking in watching Marcus squirm was not as rewarding as the anticipation that she would soon be free to openly date the son of one of the firm's owners. So she'd agreed to come to the meeting after his lawyer said Marcus capitulated — he finally agreed to her getting one-half of his yearly salary for the next five years as alimony, to pay her back for the inconvenience of having married beneath her. She expected to be the one who was smiling, once they had signed everything. Of course there would still be the one-month waiting period before the final meeting in the judge's chambers again. But after that, *Good-bye boring husband, hello moneyed single life!* She had to force herself to concentrate on what was being said when her lawyer tapped her on the arm.

"So, we are all agreed that my client will get one-half of the salary of your client for the next five years, as alimony compensation for their marriage?"

"Well, not exactly." Marcus' lawyer grinned apologetically at everyone.

"Now what?" Shandra hissed, glaring at Marcus.

"We would like the wording of the codicil to say: The party whose income exceeds that of the other party will agree to pay one-half of their yearly salary to the party whose income level is lower."

"That's what we said before." Her lawyer snapped.

"Fine, fine — word it anyway you want." Shandra was anxious to get away from Marcus and that irritating smile. "But the result will still be the same. He has to provide me with the income level I've grown used to, for the next five years."

"You are all agreed?" The judge indicated to his secretary that she needed to make the final changes to the document she was processing.

All parties involved now nodded their assent. Two copies of the divorce documents were quickly printed and placed on the table for the formality of the final signatures. Pens were produced, and the only sound was the scratching of ink-filled nibs on the papers.

With a great feeling of relief, Shandra pushed the second copy back to the judge, with both of their signatures. "Then that's all for today? Can I leave now?"

She was both surprised and irritated when Marcus' lawyer cleared his throat again. "There's just one more thing you need to be aware of, before these papers are notarized and filed."

"What? What else is there?"

Marcus smiled even more broadly than before.

Shondra balled her fists so tightly, her nails dug into her palms.

His lawyer proceeded to take out some official-looking papers from his briefcase and passed copies out to everyone in the room.

"What's this?" She was angrily scanning the papers, noting the letterhead on one sheet was from the University of Chicago Hospital System, and the other was from some place called Twin Lakes Community Hospital.

"If you will take the time to read them, madam, you will note that one is a letter of resignation, and the other is a letter of intent to take a position. Both have been witnessed, notarized, and filed in their respective counties."

Shondra glowered at Marcus and that damn smile. "What does this have to do with me?"

Frantically her lawyer pointed to the second sheet, the one from the unknown hospital, where Marcus' signature was plainly visible right under an official proposal of a job as the head of a new cardiac unit. Along with the proposal and description of the job responsibilities was the salary that was to be paid for this position. Shandra gasped and had to look twice at the number before she realized what it meant.

Marcus spoke for the first time. "You see, my dear Shandra, I plan to move up to northern Wisconsin. I don't know if I will find what I'm looking for up there, but I intend to give it a really good try. Effective the middle of June, I will no longer be employed by the University of Chicago Hospitals. I will be unemployed for a couple of weeks, then I will start the end of June at the Twin Lakes Community Hospital in Minocqua." His smile, if possible, got even wider.

She glared at him with a mixture of disbelief and dislike.

"Since they're not a world-famous teaching hospital, they're not in a major metropolitan area, and they don't have the well-connected clientele that I've been caring for until now, my salary will be drastically reduced." He cleared his throat before he continued, obviously greatly enjoying her discomfort. "So *you* will be the one who will be earning the significantly higher salary, once the divorce is final. I guess you'll be paying me one-half of your salary. But then, since I did most of the work trying to save our marriage, I'm thinking that's only fair."

"So then what happened?" Melanie asked.

They were talking again on a Tuesday night, as usual.

Marcus chuckled. "Then of course the papers were hastily revised to leave out any mention of alimony being paid by anyone. The first two copies were destroyed, and the amended papers were signed by both of us, duly witnessed, notarized, and filed with the court. The judge reminded us that he will see us again for the last time in one month. But you really should have seen her face! It was almost worth all of the aggravation she's been putting me through, just to see her face when she realized what position her greed had put her into."

"Marcus—don't you think you'll be sorry once you really have to learn to live on your new salary?"

"Honey, as long as I can live with you, I don't care what kind of money we make. And the knowledge that this whole ordeal will be over in a month is making me feel better than I have for years. And it's all because of you."

"Okay." She still didn't sound convinced.

Marcus took a deep breath before he spoke again, trying for a casual tone. "So I've been thinking that you could meet me downtown here, on the day we sign the final papers making me a free man. Then you and I can spend some time together, taking a mini-vacation. What kind of place would you like to go to? Hawaii? The Caribbean? On a cruise? If you had to pick, which would you choose?"

"That depends on the date you will be doing the final signing. I may not be done with my final grading yet."

"Let me know what date works for you, and I'll make sure the signing takes place after then. But where would you like to go, to help me celebrate?"

"Well, I've been to Florida for spring break before, but I've never been on a cruise. About the only vacations I've had involved camping with some girlfriends. I just like the idea of not having to carry money. I've heard others talk about their cruises, and the cool places they go, as well as having so much fun on the ship that they rarely get off of it."

"There's always Club Med if all you want is an all-inclusive break from reality, you know."

"Yeah, but I'd still like to see what it's like, being on a big ship. And I'll bet once the waves start tossing the ship around, you get some really good action going that would be really interesting to try—purely on a scientific basis of course." Melanie ended with a tiny purr, as if he might not have already guessed what she was referring to.

Marcus moaned. "Honey, how do you always manage to do that? Miles away, just talking about something—then you put these ideas into my head that travel right down to my dick. The next thing I know, I'll be begging you to have phone sex with me again."

"Just a gift, I guess." She giggled. "Do you want me to breathe heavy too? Maybe make some moaning noises, to simulate what I plan on sounding like, while the boat rocks us back and forth?"

"No!" He took a deep breath before continuing. "Do you care where the cruise is to? Hawaii? Alaska? The Caribbean? Mexico?" He was trying to focus and trying not to sound like the answer was as important to him as it was.

"Well, if we're only going for a couple of days, even a week, I don't think that's time enough to do justice to some place like Alaska, where I'd like to spend about a month. But we won't be able to afford that, what with your newly-reduced salary. Which reminds me, what part of this vacation am I going to be paying for? I can't expect you to foot the whole bill."

Marcus cleared his throat. "How about I just set it up and we'll worry about the details later? They do lots of cruises out of south Florida, down to Mexico and the Caribbean. June isn't a really big tourist time for them. Most folks figure it's too hot down there by then. So how about that? Sound good to you?"

"You sound like you know a lot about this." Melanie tried not to sound jealous. "You're not planning on taking me on some cruise that you were on with her, are you?"

"No! Aw, hell no! You're right about one thing—we won't be able to afford to do things *her* way. And I hope you're not really big on shopping while on vacation."

Melanie voice sounded relaxed and reassured. "No, the places I usually go, like camping in state forests, only sell tee shirts and stuff. All I really need for a good time is you in my bed, someone else does the cooking, some drinking, maybe some sight-seeing, maybe some dancing, maybe some swimming—and did I mention you in my bed?"

"Yes, you did," Marcus assured her. "And there's no place

I'd rather spend my time off either. Anywhere with you would be wonderful. But getting to share new places with you, as—" He caught himself. "As a couple, will make it even more memorable." *Careful, boy, or you're going to give too much away to her. You want to surprise her, so keep it cool.* Marcus wiped his palms on his pants before he continued. "So you'll let me know the date you will be available, then? And we'll spend a couple of nights here, downtown. I'll show you some of my favorite places around the city, then we'll fly down to Florida and start our new life together. Okay?" He held his breath, sure she would be getting suspicious by now.

But she answered in a distracted manner. "Fine, Marcus. Now I really need to go, since I have a shit-load of papers to grade. The kids have been bitching for weeks already that I need to get them done and back to them."

He groaned. "No phone sex this time?"

She laughed ruefully. "Sorry, but no. Call me on Friday, or even Saturday, and we can talk and come until we're both blue in the face, okay?"

"Okay, honey. I love you. And good night."

"I love you too, Marcus. Dream of me."

"Always. You've been my favorite dream lover for twelve years."

He's up to something. But I don't have time to think about that now. Maybe he's planning on surprising me with flowers in the state-room, or something. I'll just have to wait and see. Now on to my never-ending stacks of papers.

A couple of days later, once Melanie had e-mailed him with the date that she would be finally done with all the years' grades and free to drive down to Chicago, Marcus started to work on the details of his plan. While he ran into some initial problems, he was able to iron out all of the difficulties. The next time he called Melanie, he told her to check her e-mail for a copy of the cruise ship's itinerary, so she would know what to pack for their vacation. Then he tackled the one last problem. He tried for a casual tone "So what are you planning on wearing when you drive down here?

"I don't know. Something comfortable I guess."

"Why don't you get yourself a new summer suit with a nice blouse?" He stopped, aware that he was sounding a little bit too interested in her clothing for someone who claimed not to be metro-sexual.

"Since when have you been interested in what I was wearing, as opposed to getting me out of it?" She was only half-teasing.

He took a deep breath. "Well, I'm going to take you out to dinner right after court, since we scheduled it for late afternoon, to give you time to drive down here. The place I want to take you to caters to the very wealthy—high-society clientele. I want you to feel like you fit right in, so I can show you off to the world. And for that, you need to be dressed the part."

"Okay" She sounded doubtful. "Though I don't know where I'm going to find a *couture* suit way up here in the country." Her tone brightened. "Maybe I could get a new gingham frock?"

Marcus sighed. "Just try to find something nice. And make sure you have enough clothes packed for all of the special cruise things, like the Captain's Dinner. I can pay for some of that stuff, if you want."

"Hold on, mister!" Her voice sounded self-righteous. "There's a name for women who take money from men to buy themselves nice things, only to offer sex in return!"

"Yeah," Marcus remarked dryly, "They're called wives."

"Well, since I'm not a wife, I can buy my own clothes,

thank-you."

"Okay, okay. Forget I said anything. Show up in jeans and a tee-shirt. I'll still take you out. We do have McDonalds in the city, you know."

"Hmph! Say, does this mean if I wear a nice, pastel suit with a sexy yet demure blouse, that you will wear a suit and I can chew the tie and the shirt off of you after dinner?"

Marcus chuckled. "Of course."

"All-righty-then. I'll see what I can find and surprise you with it, okay?"

"Okay."

"Oh, and Marcus?"

"What?"

"I don't need to pack any pajamas, do I?"

He moaned. "Woman, it's not like I can ever get the thought of you naked out of my mind. Especially when I'm talking to you. Why do you have to torture me like this?"

She giggled. "Must be the devil in me. Though I'd rather have *you* in me."

"Just three more weeks, then your ass is mine!" Marcus crowed. *Uh-oh! Did I that out loud? Maybe she didn't notice.*

She hadn't. She must be too preoccupied thinking about sex, as always. "You're not the only one who is terminally horny and plagued with the image of naked, sweaty bodies. On the one hand, I wish you were up here, so I could jump you and try to get at least a little satisfied, so I could concentrate on finishing this grading I have to do. But on the other hand, I'd probably get so carried away finding new ways to please you and me that I'd never get it finished."

"So maybe we should call it a night, and both get some rest?"

"Yeah." She yawned. " I have to get at least a few more papers graded before tomorrow's first class. So, good-night, my love, and talk to you soon."

"I love you. Do some shopping. I can't wait to see you."

They both hung up the phone and went back to imagining their next meeting.

Chapter Fourteen: One Marriage Ends

Finally the school year was over. Melanie was filled with the usual sense of relief as she handed in the last of her grades for the year. Suddenly she realized that for the first time, she was really looking forward to the summer. Instead of trying to merely fill the time, she was going to spend it with Marcus! They would be looking for a place to live, since her condo was way too small for the two of them. She really needed an office in which to do the paper-grading English teachers were always so buried in. Then they would be moving in together, with the goal of being completely settled into their new place before fall. She knew Marcus was going to be learning the ropes at a new hospital also. *Lots of changes — but the most important one is that he's moving up here to live with me!*

She had already done some shopping, mostly for cruise-wear — especially a new bathing suit. But once the school year was officially ended for her, she drove to the biggest mall in the area, and after a long day spent trying on everything in her size, she finally found the suit to make Marcus happy. It was a pale cream color with a fitted skirt and jacket that made her look professional. She paired it with a coral silk blouse that enhanced her coloring and made her skin appear to glow. She also picked up some new shoes, since she could afford to wear higher heels, seeing as how Marcus was so much taller than her. *No more need to worry about whether I need flats on a date.*

It was a heady feeling to realize that she now had a man of her own and didn't have to wonder if she would be able to drag anyone back to her bed at night. So with great anticipation, she finished packing the last of her clothes and toiletries, tossed the suitcase into the passenger side of her truck, and locked up her condo to start the long drive down to Chicago.

Marcus had lots of last-minute details to take care of, so he didn't have much time during the morning to wonder how soon Melanie would arrive. Since she had called him at seven am and told him that she would be leaving soon, he estimated that she would arrive by about one or two in the afternoon. Since the final signing appointment in the judge's chambers was scheduled for three pm, he told her to drive to his condo, park there in the nearby lot, and he would get her downtown to the Civic Center.

When she wasn't there by two-fifteen, he called his brother Shawn and had him stay at the parking lot to wait for her. Marcus had to be sure to be on time so there would be no possibility of another delay, or all of his planning would have been for nothing. Then he drove himself to the Civic Center and met his lawyer there. That was when he started to worry about where Melanie was and why she was so late. He tried to call her cell phone, but she didn't answer. He had to force himself to relax, telling himself that she would be there on time.

Melanie was swearing under her breath. Not only did she hate driving in city traffic, but of course there was an accident on the highway. She had to wait in an interminable stop-and-go delay while everyone slowed down to gawk at the three cars involved. She kept looking at her watch, anxious to get to

Marcus, but knowing there was nothing she could do about it. Not being familiar with the city streets, she didn't know where to turn off to get to where she needed to be. She had to follow the map she had gotten off of the internet. She was too afraid to turn off and risk getting lost, especially since she had no idea what was a safe neighborhood. She also had to work to keep her anxiety at being in such a crowded area under control.

Her phone rang a little after two pm, but by then she was moving along again, having finally passed the accident scene. She wasn't going to risk answering her phone when she was trying to find her exit. When she finally pulled into the lot near Marcus' condo, she was surprised to see his brother Shawn leaning against a car by the entrance. She rolled her window down when he waved at her. "Hey Shawn. What are you doing here?"

"Waiting for you, beautiful!"

"Why?"

"Because Marcus had to get to the Civic Center. He asked me to wait for you and to give you a ride there. That will save some time, since I can just drop you off out front, and you won't lose time trying to find a parking space near there. Not that you would be able to find one—and you would waste a lot of time looking. Get yourself a parking lot ticket, go park your truck, and meet me back here."

"Okay, thanks." *I hope Shawn knows how to get to the right judge's chambers. I don't want to waste time wandering around the Civic Center looking for a judge whose name I don't even know.* Finding a parking space took a bit of time, since it was the middle of the afternoon on a weekday. Many of the available spaces were too small for her truck. She chose not to take the elevator down, but ran down the stairs, two at a time, from the sixth floor. "I'm here. Let's go!" She was panting as she got into Shawn's car.

"I sure wish you were panting with excitement at seeing

me again. I just might be tempted to kidnap you instead of taking you to the Civic Center. That way I could keep you for myself."

Since he had teased her like this when she had last seen him, ten years ago, she didn't worry about whether or not he was serious. She knew that Marcus trusted him implicitly, or he would not have asked him to wait for her. "Just get me to the Civic Center on time. God, I hate driving in Chicago traffic." She proceeded to spend the short drive telling him all about the accident, the stop-and-go traffic she had been stuck in — and just for good measure, how much she really hated driving in large metropolitan areas.

"Yea, I get that!" Shawn grinned when she finally stopped. "Marcus reminded me that you rarely stop to breathe once you get going talking. I thought he must be exaggerating, but now I realize he wasn't. The passing of time hasn't slowed you down at all, has it?"

"Ha ha! You're older than me, as I remember, so enough of that. Hey, do you know where I need to go in the Civic Center?"

Shawn told her the directions, and she wrote them down to be sure she didn't get lost. When he dropped her off at the front of the building, she quickly jumped out of the car, yelling "Thanks!" She found the correct elevator and got up to the right floor in enough time to have about fifteen minutes to go until three p.m. *Just enough time to use the bathroom and to check to be sure I look all right.*

Five minutes later she was powdering her nose when she realized that a woman had entered the bathroom and was just standing there, staring at her.

"Excuse me, do I know you?" She turned to face the other woman.

"No. But I know who you are. I've seen your picture. You don't look as good in person."

"Hmm, let's see — beautiful Black woman, expensive taste

in clothes, perfectly groomed — you must be Shandra."

"Yes. And you're the slut who stole my man."

Melanie sighed. "First of all, I didn't steal Marcus. You had already thrown him out before he got in touch with me again. I hadn't seen him in ten years."

"But I notice that you don't deny that you're a whore. And not even a very good one, since you never got paid for it."

Melanie smiled in spite of herself. "Obviously you're expecting me to be hurt by your calling me names. But I'm okay with the kind of woman I was then, just like I'm okay with who I am now. But what's probably bothering you more is that Marcus is okay with the way I was then and the way I am now. I don't really care what your opinion is."

"But you did take my man away from me. He might still be my husband if you hadn't committed adultery with him. He might have tried to work things out with me. But you made it too easy for my man to leave."

Taking a deep breath, Melanie shook her head. "No, not really. What you're forgetting is that Marcus was *never* really *your man* to begin with, no matter how you tried to lay claim to him. Marcus has been *my man* for over twelve years. He's just come back to me after a really long break."

"You lying bitch!" Shandra's voice was getting louder. "The investigator told me that *you* were the one who broke up with him. You laid him low, and now you're back to do it again."

"No. Now I realize how wrong I was to let him go. And I'm staking claim again to what belongs to me."

Melanie didn't get to hear what was going to come out of Shandra's mouth next, since the door was abruptly thrown open.

Another impeccably groomed woman stepped in and looked around. "Shandra! There you are. We need to get into the judge's chambers now."

With a final angry glare, Shandra turned and strode out of the bathroom.

Melanie leaned against the sink and breathed a sigh of relief. In a pissing contest, she was really afraid that Shandra could out-insult her. They both spoke for a living, basically, but Shandra was in her element here, in a courthouse. And despite how much money she'd spent on her suit, Melanie couldn't help but feel that compared to the other women, she looked shabby. She shook herself, taking one final look in the mirror to try to bolster her confidence, telling her reflection, "He chose me over her. I was right. He's *my* man!" Then she walked resolutely out of the door.

Marcus was in the hall striding up and down the length of it. Looking almost frantic with worry, he quickly raced over to her. "Melanie! Where have you been? Shawn told me about the traffic accident that slowed you down, but he called me over ten minutes ago, to say he had dropped you off out front." He folded her into his arms, for a close hug, then he tilted her face up, to give her a quick kiss.

Melanie responded to his touch with a sigh, enjoying the feeling of being wrapped in his arms. She snuggled closer and spoke into his chest. "I was slightly delayed in the bathroom by a beautiful woman who accused me of stealing her husband. I believe you know her?" She looked up into his face.

Marcus regarded her gravely. "And what did you say to her?"

She smiled. "I told her that despite what she thought, you never belonged to her. That you have been *mine* for over twelve years."

He smiled back at her, lifting her face up to gaze into her eyes. "You're right, honey. I've been your man since the first time you took pity on a poor, skinny, under-nourished boy and made all of his dreams come true. Now let's go into the judge's chambers and fix this mistake of mine, so we can do things right from now on."

Holding his hand, and now feeling decidedly much less shabby, Melanie proudly walked by his side into the room where his divorce would be finalized.

CHAPTER FIFTEEN: AND A NEW LIFE BEGINS

Twenty minutes later, Shandra and her lawyer walked out of the room without a backward glance at anyone. Marcus shook hands with his lawyer, thanking him for his hard work. Then the lawyer left the room. Melanie noticed that Marcus was not looking relieved—if anything, he had looked calmer before. Now he looked positively nervous. He turned to the judge, asking, "Can we have a couple of minutes, alone?"

The judge smiled at him. "Of course. Just give a holler out the door when you need me back in here." With that cryptic comment, he smiled at Melanie and turned to go out into the hallway.

Aghast, Melanie asked, "Did you just throw the judge out of his own chambers?"

Marcus cleared his throat before answering. "Not throw, technically. I'd asked him ahead of time if I could have a few minutes alone with you, after the divorce was finalized and I was once again a free man."

Melanie looked at him in surprise. "Why?" She was even more shocked when he got down on one knee before her and took her hands in his.

"This is why," he answered, huskily. He used one hand and drew a tiny box out of his jacket pocket. He opened it, and she saw two multi-colored gold rings. "Melanie, we can always exchange the rings for other ones, if you don't like them. But will you make me the happiest man in the world and marry me?"

"Of course I will! You know I will!" She had tears in her eyes. "I love you, Marcus. And this time I'm not too scared to say *yes*. Now that you're a free man, we can start planning on getting married as soon as possible."

"I don't think you understand me yet, honey. I mean *now*. Will you marry me now — here, in the judge's chambers? I asked you once before and you said *No*. I'm not taking any chances anymore. I'm not giving you any time to change your mind or to get scared again. I want you to decide if you can do this *now*, so that when you walk out of the judge's chambers, it will be as my wife!"

Realization came over her as she stared into his eyes. "Is this why you were so concerned about what I wore?"

He grinned sheepishly. "Yes. I didn't think you would forgive me if you wore something casual and that was what would be in the pictures hanging on our wall for the rest of our lives. The children would ask us *How come Mama didn't dress up to marry you, Daddy?* And we'd have to explain to them that I tricked you into saying *yes*, because I was determined not to let you go ever again!"

She tried unsuccessfully to glare at him. Instead she found, to her embarrassment, that tears were forcing themselves to her eyes, and she had to look at him through them. "You sneak!" was all she managed to choke out before a sob broke through her reserves.

"Honey! What's the matter? Don't cry. Just tell me, yes or no?"

"Ye-esss!" She burst into tears. All the pent-up frustration of trying to be there on time, along with the tension of feeling out-classed by his ex-wife and her lawyer — all was washed away with the sheer joy of knowing that he wanted her so much that he had arranged this to surprise her.

"Yes!" he repeated loudly. He strode quickly over to the

door, opened it, and yelled into the hall, "Yes! She said *Yes!*"

Suddenly the room filled with people. First came the judge, then Marcus' mother, his brother Shawn, and his other siblings. They all crowded around Melanie, welcoming her to the family.

His mother hugged her closely, whispering into her ear, "It's about time, dear!" She winked and smiled at Melanie and gave her back to Marcus.

The door opened again, and Melanie was surprised to see her parents walk in, followed by her brother and his wife.

"Surprise!" they all yelled, as more hugs were exchanged.

Her mom was already crying, explaining to Melanie, "Remember, I always cry at weddings because they make me so happy."

Melanie turned to glare at Marcus, "You planned all of this?"

He smiled innocently. "Would you have forgiven me if your parents weren't at your wedding? I don't think so."

"We're all staying at the same hotel down here. What a place!" Melanie's brother Tom was obviously impressed.

His wife Joanne smiled, nodding. "It's like a second honeymoon for us. We could never afford a stay there, but Marcus insisted we all be together."

Melanie turned to look at Marcus. "What would you have done if I said *No*?"

He turned to the judge. "Start now! She's going to change her mind again. Somebody lock the door! Let's get this marriage thing done. I'm not letting her out of this room until we're married."

Everyone laughed, while the judge assumed his place in front of his desk and asked for quiet. While he got ready to recite the words of the marriage ceremony, Melanie and Marcus found themselves looking into each other's eyes.

"No doubts this time?" he asked her gently.

"No. Are you sure this will be legal?"

He smiled. "The judge is one of my ex-patients. I worked it all out with him ahead of time. Once he says we're married, you are *so* not getting away from me!"

She smiled back. "Good! And neither are you. I only plan to marry once. This is it for you, buddy. You'd better really mean it this time. When he says forever, that's how long I'm holding on to you."

"Ahem." The judge cleared his throat to get their attention. Everyone in the room was quiet as he began to say the words that would bind Marcus and Melanie together.

Melanie found that she was so choked up that she had trouble repeating the words that were required of her. Marcus appeared to be having the same trouble. But they got through what they needed to say and exchanged the rings that Marcus had picked out for them.

At this point in the ceremony, Melanie expected it to end; so she was surprised when the judge stopped and nodded at Marcus.

Marcus took a piece of paper out of his pocket. Turning to everyone gathered there he explained. "I want to finish this ceremony by reading a poem that Melanie wrote and sent to me when we found each other again." He turned to look into Melanie's eyes. "I took the liberty of adding two lines at the end—I'll give you this copy when it is your turn to say your last two lines." He started to read—

After all of these years I have spent alone,
With no love to call my own,
I wonder more than you can ever know,
If I was wrong to let you go.
Now, after just one dance,
I have hope that for us, there is a second chance.
You pledge to me, and I pledge to you,
Forever, may our love be true.

He looked into her eyes, saying softly,
I will be your husband and you my wife,
I will love and care for you for the rest of my life.

He handed her the paper and waited for a moment while she cleared her throat, trying to read through her tears. She looked into his eyes, to say in a strong voice the words he had written for her.
You will be my husband and I your wife,
I will love and care for you for the rest of my life.
The silence of the room was marred only by the soft sobbing of Melanie's mom.

The judge broke the silence. "If there are no objections, I now declare you husband and wife." Noticing that Marcus and Melanie had not moved and were still gazing into each other's eyes, he cleared his throat. "You may now kiss the bride. Marcus, kiss her already."

"Mine! All mine!" Marcus pulled Melanie into his arms for a kiss that seemed to represent all of the years of longing, of waiting for this moment. They pressed their lips together, their tongues swept into each other's mouths, and they both groaned as they melded their bodies together, oblivious to the assembled witnesses.

Marcus' mom was the one to break the silence, using a sheet of paper to fan herself. "Lordy, Lordy, boy, have the decency to hold off on consummatin' this until you have fed us all some dinner!"

Everyone laughed, glad of a release from the tension of watching as Melanie and Marcus heated up the room.

Reluctantly, Marcus let go of his new wife, turning sheepishly to smile at their families.

His mother grabbed Melanie in a big hug. "Welcome to the family, honey. Where you belong.""

Melanie's mother hugged Marcus. "You did it! You surprised her, and you got her to marry you. Congratulations!"

"Welcome, son." Melanie's father shook hands with Marcus warmly.

Melanie's brother and sister-in-law were the next ones hugging Marcus.

Shawn grabbed Melanie for a dramatic kiss, but stopped when Marcus tapped his shoulder and made a menacing fist.

"Hey, you'll never let me kiss her again. I figured I'd better take my chance when I could."

Marcus' other siblings hugged Melanie also, with the men careful not to invite the wrath of Marcus, who was now watching them all closely, making sure that no one took undue liberties with his wife.

Melanie turned to him, laughing at his attitude. "Hey, we're married now, dude. You don't have to worry about me anymore. Like I said, I'm only doing this once. You had your chance to get away from me — you didn't take it. You're stuck with me now. No amount of good-looking men hugging me is going to change that."

He reclaimed her then, pulling her to his side and possessively grabbing her ass as he turned to glare at his brothers. "No more! Keep your hands off. She's mine."

Everyone laughed as they all crowded out the door. Marcus had rented stretch limos to take them all to dinner at the top of the Prudential, where he had booked a private room for them to celebrate in while they ate, drank, and made merry.

Hours later, Melanie giggled as Marcus swept her into his arms and carried her across the threshold of the Newlyweds suite he had booked for them. Looking around at the opulent surroundings, she gasped. "Are you sure we can afford to stay here? You're not going to be making the kind of money that you used to, you know."

He smiled smugly at her. "You have no idea what kind of money I have been making. This doesn't even begin to make a dent in what I'm worth. You married well, my dear. Get used to it."

"And you put my family up in two other rooms in this place?"

"Yes, but not special suites. They're in smaller rooms, a couple of floors beneath us."

"Oooh," she moaned. "A couple of floors beneath us? So they won't hear me when I scream? How thoughtful."

She moved closer to him and began to rub herself on him, grabbing his ass and kneading it while she moved up and down, pressing against his throbbing erection. "I wonder what I can do to thank you for this wonderful wedding surprise. Can you think of anything, or is your brain too short on blood supply to make any suggestions?"

He groaned. "Woman, I've managed to get divorced from the wrong wife and married to the right wife, all in one day. I've made nice with your family and mine. I've paid for everything. Now it's time to reckon up. Either you get naked in the next five seconds, or I'm going to chew your nice new suit off and ravish you until you scream and beg for mercy! And since we're married now, I'm not using condoms anymore."

"Promises, promises!" She laughed as she clawed at his suit.

He tore off her clothing. "It's not consummated yet. We're not really married until it is. So let's get to it!"

And they did. Over and over. Hours later, they ended up, as they always had before, in the tub. This one was as oversized as the room—a king-sized *Jacuzzi* with plenty of water for them to slosh all over the floor.

The End

NOTE

There is indeed only one hospital in Minocqua, Wisconsin, but it is not called Twin Lakes Community Hospital. I don't know anything about their hospital, but I didn't find cardiac care listed on their departmental listings. For the sake of my book, since I love camping in the area up by Minocqua, I made up a hospital name and personnel. If you want to find an area less touristy than the Dells, but with great camping at the fourteen campgrounds in the two State Forests there, with fishing, swimming and other outdoor sports in an ideal setting, I advise you to join Marcus and head up to Minocqua, Wisconsin.

You may also enjoy the following from eXtasy Books Inc:

Worth the Wait
Fiona McGier

Excerpt

"Why did they ask you?" Grant asked, closely watching his mother, Gertrude, as she sat behind her oak desk.

This office on the first floor of the house he'd grown up in was where she took care of all the family businesses. There were many pictures of him at various ages, along with his siblings. A large portrait sat behind her. It showed her as a young woman on her wedding day, smiling as she held the hand of the young man who was her husband. Grant was always amused by that. Though he was one of the older kids, even he couldn't remember their father's hair as blond. It had turned gray at a young age, a silver color that made him look much older than he was until he actually grew older.

Gertrude shrugged. "Who knows? Maybe because we're known to them, since we've done business together? Maybe because we were just there, and that reminded Diego of our special skill set?"

His younger brother, Glen, stroked his heavy beard and snorted. "Or maybe he wants one of us around in case there's any future trouble? Changes in pack leadership can cause lots of unrest until things settle down. And we've got a track record of helping them clean up their messes."

Gertrude pursed her lips in disapproval. "Glen, stop. We've enjoyed their hospitality many times when we've wanted a change of location for a holiday. They've always been glad to host us, either all together, or in smaller groups. Why shouldn't we be called when they have problems that they know we can take care of for them?"

The door was thrown open, and a force of nature entered. Grant's oldest sibling, his sister Griselda, swept into the room. "Hi. Sorry I'm late. Couldn't be helped. What'd I miss?"

Guy, another brother with a beard, snickered. "Take too long kissing goodbye?"

She shot a withering look at their youngest brother. "No, Guy. I was talking with his mother when I got the text from Mom. And I don't generally kiss his mother at all . . . if I can help it."

Smiles traveled around the room. Everyone was used to the bickering that ran through the fabric of their familial relationships.

Gertrude explained. "Seems that the Northern Maine Pack leadership has need of a temporary replacement for one of their ranking members. Remember John, Joe's second child, and only son? He's been their second in command, so the head of their security, ever since he got old enough and strong enough to do the job. But he's taking a leave for a while, and they'll need someone to replace him."

"For how long?" Grant asked.

"I don't know. I don't think they know, either. I got the impression from Diego that this is kind of sudden, and not something he's happy about. Like Glen said, pack leadership change can be very unsettling, especially for a pack that's been under the same leader for damn near sixty years. Having another change so soon is adding another layer of uncertainty. I think he's trying to minimize the number of people who are aware of what's been going on within their ranks. So asking us to send someone to help out is a no-brainer, since we're already known to them."

"But we're not very good at following orders," Griselda pointed out, wearing a grin. "We're all kind of independent. Our family crest says Doesn't play well with others."

Gertrude sighed. "I know. That's what I told him. But I said I'd check with my brood to see if any of you might be interested. He's got a couple of packs he's in contact with that he can ask next. But we were the first ones he called."

"Well, I'm out," Griselda said with a toss of her white-blond hair. "I'm not about to leave town and have my man be prey to other females while I'm not here to fend them off."

Gertrude nodded. "That's what I figured you'd say."

"Can't let up the pressure now, huh, sis? Almost got him ready to propose? Be a shame if all of that work you've done on him, softening him up, made him ready to get married, then some other woman was closer than you when he worked up the nerve to propose."

Guy ducked as the accurately named throw-pillow flew his way.

"I'm not interested," said Glen. "I've got more clients than I can deal with already. I don't trust any of my partners enough to let them handle the ins and outs of my business."

Guy added, "And I just got a contract to photograph the effects of climate change on polar bears, so I'm headed up to the great white north in the very near future. Like, in a week or so."

Gertrude turned to him. "Grant?"

He appeared to be considering his words before speaking.

"I might be interested. I was talking with Nathan, their fourth, over dinner when we were there. He said it was too bad that their leader's wife was heading out of town, because she and I would have a lot to talk about. Her degree is in biological research, and she's been trying to isolate and identify possible markers in the blood to see if there's any way to predict which young ones will discover they're shifters when their hormones turn on."

Glen grinned. "I think it's pretty obvious when they fall on the ground and their bones start cracking and shifting around. Yup, that one's got a wolf inside trying to get out."

"But not before that," Grant stressed. "Lots of people send their kids to the Maine Academy for high school because they don't know if their kids will present or not . . . or when. If there was a way to predict it, parents would at least have the peace of mind of knowing their kids were in a safe place for their first time."

"Wouldn't that mean fewer people would send their kids to the academy?" Griselda asked.

"I wondered about that, too. But Nathan said their belief is that they might actually end up with even more applicants. Right now, some are willing to chance that it won't happen, and sometimes it's a disaster when it does. This way, they would know for sure."

"It does tend to run in families, but that's not really dependable. Your father and I were both shifters, and all of you are also. But then there's Joe and Janine's Jennifer. Both her parents were shifters, and she's the oldest. But no wolf inside of her."

Grant nodded, agreeing with his mother. "That's right."

She regarded him closely. "So you're volunteering? What about your job?"

He shrugged. "I've been kind of unhappy at work lately. Running a lab is not what I expected. Having to produce results that the client wants, instead of what actually happens, is totally bogus. I've actually been considering going back to earn my doctorate, but I'm not even sure what I'd want to get it in."

"I always thought you were heading towards being a medical doctor," Glen said with a wink. "All of those pretty nurses to toady to your every whim."

Another pillow thrown by Griselda hit him in the face, and

he pretended to be wounded. "Ow! Mom, did you see what she did? Tell her to quit throwing things around."

Gertrude glared sternly at Griselda, her lips twitching in amusement. "Grisel, stop abusing your brothers."

Griselda stuck her tongue out at Glen. "Sexist!"

He laughed. "You're so easy to bait, sis!"

"Besides," Guy pointed out, "the last time I was in the hospital, when I had my appendix removed, many of the nurses were men."

Grant chuckled. "I'm pretty sure I'll eventually become a doctor — or maybe a nurse. But I got too burned out by years of classes. I needed a break. That's why I've been working these past few years. Maybe I just need another change of scenery. And the chance to work in the lab with Mrs. Vargas, trying to do something useful with the skills that I already have? It's a tempting addition to just being able to live somewhere else for a while."

"Just be sure it's only in the lab that you want to work closely with her," Guy teased. "Diego might be injured, but he's not the kind of man to take kindly to anyone flirting with his wife."

Grant grimaced. "Not my type. That red hair could stop traffic. Besides, I don't like my women to be whiter than my ass. I'm not even sure that's possible, but I'm not interested in finding out."

Griselda snickered. "I keep telling you boys, y'all need to do some nude sunbathing."

She managed to duck all three pillows thrown her way.

Gertrude shook her head at everyone. "Fine. I'll let Diego know that you'll be heading down there. When? After you give two weeks' notice at the lab?"

He tried to look sheepish. "Um, actually I gave notice last week. I only have to work until Friday, then I'm free."

Glen got up, stretching. "So, is this family meeting adjourned? I haven't eaten since early this morning, and I'm not going to make it until dinner unless I grab some kind of snack."

Guy headed toward the door. "Race you to the kitchen! Loser has to cook."

Griselda was already pounding down the hall, yelling behind her. "I call not cleaning up either!"

Gertrude shook her head, turning her attention to him.

"Kids," he said, rolling his eyes.

"You're really serious? You'll go? What if it gets extended into a longer visit?"

"You mean if John decides not to come back?"

She nodded.

"I guess I'll cross that bridge when and if it happens. They'll probably bump everyone else up a notch, so that'll make me the fourth. They can always promote someone from their security ranks if that happens. We'll see. But either way, I'm out of a job and need a change and a new challenge. This is just what I've been waiting for." He got up. "I'm feeling kind of peckish, too. I'm going to see what they're rustling up in the kitchen."

"You do that," Gertrude said. "And I'll call Diego back."

He stopped at the door to blow her a kiss, before heading toward the noise coming from the kitchen.

It wasn't until much later that night, after having eaten dinner and gone home to bed, that Grant listened to his wolf berate him.

Why didn't you let them know that we claim her?

Instantly, he was swept along on the current of lust his wolf had felt the last time he was at the Maine compound. He'd been slammed by a tidal wave of emotions when a large black she-wolf appeared in front of them. She had put her body directly in front of the two renegade wolves, thereby protecting the pack leader and his wife. He smiled, wondering what the female might look like as a human. As a wolf, she was enticing enough.

I can't do that. If my brothers even suspected we were

interested in her, their competitive instincts would take over, and they'd want to fight us for her.

His wolf snarled softly in his mind. *You always underestimate our abilities. We are the oldest. We are the strongest. We would win any battle.*

I won't fight my own brothers that fiercely. I won't hurt either of them. It's better this way, you'll see. They'll be miles away, and we can slowly approach the female so as not to scare her off.

Why not let me approach her wolf? It would be quicker. Wolves mate as they will, with no time wasted in what you call courtship.

I want to capture her human self also. As you say, the wolf part of her will be easy to convince. It's the human I have to encourage to see me — us — as her mate.

Temporarily mollified, his wolf quieted down. And Grant took matters into his own hands, relieving the pressure of their yearnings.

About the Author

Mom taught me to read when I was five. Since then, I have always had characters intruding into my thoughts, showing scenes from their lives. When I ignore them, they start to yell louder. If I write their stories so they can live in readers' heads as well, they usually leave me alone . . .until the next voices appear. I like the noise.

Learn more about me and my books, read excerpts and reviews, at www.fionamcgier.com

Or come visit me on Facebook:

https://www.facebook.com/fiona.mcgier/

www.ingramcontent.com/pod-product-compliance
Lightning Source LLC
Chambersburg PA
CBHW070933130626
46555CB00001B/417